THE SAUSAGE. THE END. THE WORLD.

www.rafaelspringer.com

Printed by: Books on Demand GmbH, Norderstedt

ISBN 978-2-9599737-3-4

RAFAEL SPRINGER

THE SAUSAGE. THE END. THE WORLD.

CLOCKING TIME

To the troublemakers, home-comers and terminators…

All of it! Too much. All of it! Too far. Time. It passes. Too fast! Pitilessly. Seeps. Melts. Away! Deepens. In thoughtlessness. Ridiculously! Always they come. In between! The troublemakers à gogo. No day without opportunity. Missed. Naked. Desire. Blank envy! The annihilating inferiority. A must! Those force-fed seconds. Of sausaged time. Tiresome remains of a big bang. Of a quirky fate. With two knotted ends. Emergency exit: forget it! Teeth biting them? Cannot do it. Do not want it! Divine teeth? Divinity fudge? It, time, flowing through genes too tight. Manipulated! Stuttering ones! Scary ones! Petty ones! Temporary ones! And, nevertheless, scarcely to be cut off. Possibilities to escape? None. The knots are too good! Pulled too tight. Death. The end. Of the sausage. The closer to the end of this sausage, the tighten the knots. And in between? Greasy time splashes. Atomic transient mushrooms. Ceasing to be. With one depression after the other. The low kick of the addiction. Of the daily prognosis. Weather forecasts. Traffic jam predictions. 5.15 pm. The time is ripe. The day flees. The weather channels are stoking up. The ones with a depression over the Bay of Cologne. The others with a high on the Alzette[1]. I am the

[1] Tributary river of the Sauer. Flows through Luxemburg.

Alzette. No real river. No clear one. Am also no clear person. No clear thinker. Streamlined. No story writer. No taleteller. No sensemaker. Let the others talk fluently. I cannot do it. Do not want it. Not so! Not now! Not here! No time. No lust. It doesn't make sense. I knot them together! The bars of this book. Like ramsausages. Like wordsausages. Desecrate them. Toss them. Crunch them. In my head. In my paws. My being! Like defenceless sperms in the knot of a condom. The cusp of desire. The corner of the pinching fun. Carry on with them. Drive it out. Of them. What was said. For fun. And the not speakable? Throw it flatly on the stretcher of innocence. The bleached rain forest discs. Black on white. Binary. Recently. The stammering sponge cells protest. The wobbly stem cells too. Let them! Go ahead! Stutter! Laugh! Wonder! In my solitary confinement cell I am the boss! Alone! With time. Only play a role. Extra's leading role. Roll forwards. In the deadlock! I am time, I am cannon fodder. Rifle heel! Loaded! Ready to shoot. Playing affected? Not that bad. It will come out all right! The experts agree. An irretrievable end? There is none. No irretrievable end? None. Anyhow. The time's chance of survival is jammed. In the stanchions of the sausages of life's meat. Its healing would be a miracle. A scandal. An illusion. Another one. In the current monotony. Time has come. Is a sausage. The Alzette is a sausage. A cracking one. Losing itself in the blow-out sausage. In the glowing fat. In the expanding one. In no time! Oops? Speed limit? Dead loss! Sounds like a sensation. On the run.

Of the interchangeable Alzette. This grilled river. In time-lapse motion. Escape in the affected seas. Dragging the time tankships on the back. A heavy load! With double bottom. And lovely name. Erika! The seas which languidly pull their floods over their tides. Like the dreamer the duvet over his greedy sleep. This cramped time traveller! Accepted in the club of the stingy tides. And that in any and every night. Seas which lengthen me in my Alzette. Like a tasteless chewing gum. Bitten and spat out. If needs be to New York. Stretched. In length. Where it devours the dust of the twin towers. It! The tasteless. Timeless! The accidental time scratch ticket in a starved gambling game. Zero chance of winning. Soaked hours. Lying seconds. Bogus sessions of life. In the meat. Of the sausage. That dangles on me. Between the Alzette and the Hudson River. They, the knot sticks of the Atlantic Ocean. That lets the time tankers scarify crooked pregnancy scars into the skin. As if it was the beginning of a gaga town in the curve of a sharp night. But not with me! The distance is too big. Between both ends. The sausage too long. The meat too stinky. Time gone to seed. Decay smells. The sausage a rivulet. An Alzette. A knotted. Brewed one. That backs up. And does not dare. Dare to rise. Flood danger in the deep valley of the past. The pregnancy tears. And the future? Stuck. Cooked and stirred. It's not me! Is out of the question. Am no natural gut. You got it? Only to make sure. Where it leads? Whether the knot bursts? If out-of-nothing comes out of nothing? Like the sausage palaces out of the Alzette valley. The valley of falling and befalling. And it would also please you. Of that I am convinced. The life in another city. More life. More people. More time. More bearing. More fermenting. More prospering. Only the temperature must be right. And the automatic time. The adjustable. The atomic one. So that it does not burn! The imbued. Sluggish. Misdoing. The inanimated dangling in the gut skins. Between the continents. The time in the meatgrinder. Strained. The time atoms in the sausage. Hidden. The Alzette in sheep's clothing. Crawling away. The moaning in my forehead. Arrived. My eyes like knots. Tautologised. Two blond pigtails in the freeze-frame of my reflection which swims in the black coffee cup. And threatens to drown. My future! In the morass of the coffee grounds. Drowned. A blunt bludgeoning. However, the look gets a motionless fright. Mine. The sucked one. What is that? How does it look? Does it smell? That's not how it goes! My knot is unravelable after all! Imprisoned in it. In the coffee knot. Dispute knot. Hourly knot. The hours are nerves. Counted. Incorporated ones. The thoughts traffic knots. Enervating! Knockouts! Flashing traffic jam lights in the roadmap of my confusion. Watch out! Important message! Because of large mob of people increased traffic jam danger on the Adolphe Bridge. Honking cars devour unsuspecting home-comers. Bearing beer in mind. Logging-off. Enervated. What if the children scream? Or the wife? Or the conked-out washing machine? The mailbox jams? The bills wedged in it? The neighbour is visiting? Or even the parents-in-law? And their dog? Or winter sets in? And night constantly falls? Into our life. One hour too early? A season too early? This confuses. Blackens the mood. Of expectations. Which? Well those, if you wait and it does not come. The imagined. The ordered one. And what if it is not so? The children only want to play? The wife only wants to love? The washing machine only washes? It changes nothing in the everyday traffic jam. In the traffic knots. The thought knots. On the Adolphe Bridge. On the Brooklyn Bridge. And in my life? Does the flowing of the Alzette change if the bridge has two ends? Piled-up ones. That of the Hudson River? Probably not! A bridge is a sausage. Whether here or there. With knotted top and bottom. And the home-comers are meat mash. All over! Exploitable meat clots in packaged megalomania. Dressed up phallus imitations. Whether skin and bones are also processed in the sausages? Like in the home-comers? Like chicken feathers in chocolate? Is our time fed with useless traffic jam? With toxic queues? In a town out of time. Time equals straightjacket. In the spunk of madness. In the queue of cars. That atomizes itself. In me. Has it also come too soon? Like nightfall. Gone astray. Deeply cut. And bleeding. Dark red drops lose themselves in braking lights. Burning lava in the decline. Of the sun. Blushed rigor. If you look into her eyes. Deep-sea diver vistas. If at all? You see anything. In the booze of time. Boozed bashfulness. Moulding melancholy. Crawling into the home-comers. Creeping into the traffic jams. Debarks into the car-home-comers, frenzied hoots lulling themselves into a fool's paradise. In a car sausage chain. Jammed. Like in tinny arrogance. The time of the Adolphe Bridge! Caged. Unscrupulously managed by traffic jam reporters. 5.15 pm. Receive secret information! From future home-comers. Bogged down offshoots. Screaming smart-asses. Steady on! Not over there! It jams! Tremendous! Using detours! Absolutely! Locating catastrophic traffic conditions. There is no way forward and none back. We are to believe that? Of course! Become afraid. Know undercover detours. Otherwise it's your shot. Then take these! These hidden paths. Oases of the emergency exits proclaimed by radio waves. Knowledges of the useless obtained free of charge. We are to spin loops. To drop mucus spoors. But not to reach the target. That must not be the issue. The bridge would be the way. Hell? Sorry? The end of the sausage would be a contracted tied condom? Hell? This sluggish lappet of a ticking civilization. Well-behaved and clockwise. Trail it behind us? The time. Of the traffic jam. Hell? Leave dragging spoors? Absolutely! As indication. Of life. And the mothers will scream: Good boy! Another such loop, there he bends on home straight. The spectators can already see him. Oops! He looks around, a home-comer from France only just catches up with him. On the home straight line! But what is that? Time has broken away from him. Traffic jam swallowed him. Exhausted. Unhappy. Deterred. Is there yet something else? The traffic jam of the life clock runs off. Ticking! So here it is where the seconds disappear! And? Do you like it? You are not looking at all! Don't you care how they mutiny? They buckle? Under the load of the unspeakable? Yet however they are running out my stock, the seconds! I must do it. Speak it out. Try it. But only in order to make sure! That it does not disappear. This accumulated time feeling. Above this unmistakeable Alzette valley. That is actually an entirely different one. This tiresome traffic jam feeling. Upon this cheapish Adolphe Bridge. That steadily and gradually crumbles. Shakes. Under the constant load. Of the seconds. Of the confusions. Of the waiting. Of the bored dreaming. Of the eternal home-comers. And their shamelessly kicked footsteps. On the brakes. The clutches. The sidewalk. On the spat-out chewing gums. The feet of the others. The spit of the others. Steps of anger. Steps of impatience. Steps in the fix. Of the perspiring feet. Of the others. Steps in their footfalls. Must crush them together. I. These steps. And their thoughts! So that they do not crack and bang. Like firecrackers or peas in the universe of their vehicles and their ready-made shoes. To kill the time. However, does the time strike? Down? Back? Around itself? Around us? Around me? That's none of its concern. As usual. And of mine? I strike back. Yeah! Why not? "I'll be back!" Slogans against the trespass. Of time! David against Goliath. Alzette against Hudson River. Adolphe Bridge against Brooklyn Bridge. Terminator against Terminauthor. It runs down the pan. Like words down a book. Like thoughts down the beads of sweat. Like slobber down the anonymous traffic jam indicators. To surrender without a fight? By no means! To heck with it! The trap. The pleasure. Taken in time. Killed in action. Taken in war. Of senseless stars. Of these crazed witnesses of time. Of this cinema screen for beginners. Dream beginners. Timekeepers. Time-enmeshers. Of the ropes for gibbeted clocks! Molten ones. Dali's clocks! Is this clear now? I don't think so. But all the same. Only the last deadline is sure: Now and here. On the Adolphe Bridge. In the daily traffic jam. In the passing time of the poor devils. On the way into deserved peace. Of the evening. It is a battlefield. Home advantage. For now. Absolutely! Yeah! The least I expect. Another field is not available. At the moment! I like it. I enjoy fighting with shadows. Trick number one: Pugilism! Shadows do not box back. Are too sissy. And passing days cast their shades ahead. In pointless footsteps. Gestures from yesterday. Tramplings of herds. Terrible crush. I require personal protection. Indemnity. Extra time. Penalty shoot-out. Want a new sensation of time. Any feeling at all. A timeframe. Timeretainer. In order to adjust the teeth of the feelings. Rightly. With which I could fight. Nevertheless! What if it exceeds my strength? If I am no Terminator? No watches-bending Dali? No time melter? Only an ambiguous reasoner. Unequivocal unreasoner. Someone confused. Someone coming home. Someone lost in the sloshed traffic jam. Someone shitty in lost identity. Someone withering in time. An indecent mass murderer. Of the mass words. Well annotated! One among many. One like no one. One more or less. One is too much. One must leave. One has to be topped. Get me out of here, I am a hero! Do I clamour! Do I think! Do you believe! However, faith does not move bridges. Only mountains. And no screams either. And mountains devour time. But only sometimes. Bulimia! And time proliferates. Uncontrollably. Destroying. Without exception. And mountains are seeking refuge in valleys. Screams in heads. Always! And valleys below bridges. Mostly! Exclamations in point! Ready is the sausage! Save that Adolphe remains a dopey bridge. Across the ridiculous Alzette. Oops! Something is wrong there. Oops! The Alzette is not the Hudson River. Is the Petrusse[2]. Adolphe is not Brooklyn. You not I. But what's the difference. In this squall of words. This narrationless jumble of the collapsing sentences. Of the accumulating words. Of the lolloped mental leaps. Springer is yarning! But oops! The truth concerns nobody. Me least. Alzette? Petrusse? Adolphe? Brooklyn? All of them sausages with knotted ends. Don't scratch the sleeping sausage at the wrong end! And if you are stuck in the daily traffic jam of Brooklyn Bridge and praying for heavenly assistance in this stop-and-go human mash and exactly in this time slot this Terminator knocks in implausible distress on your insect-killing-windshield and blubbers: "GET ME OUT OF HERE!", does it then make a difference which water flows under which bridge? Or which home-comer is jammed in which tinny straightjacket? In which words the story gets entangled? In the traffic jam you are always

[2] Tributary river of the Alzette. Flows through Luxemburg.

subjugated. To a worldwide sect of pious mass homecomers. A devout contemporary witness of dead beat globalization. Of time. Indeed? As you see. How quick it can go. How quick Intifada warriors creep out of harmless motherfuckers. Like the maggots off the fat. Chimeras off the brain. And then a mummed Terminator creeps by the only gap in the time window into your safe car. Or into your blurred story. Like an unwept tear backwards through the tear duct into the jam of a dam. And starts to howl like a damned sissy. Oops! Does it then make no difference to his tears whether they end in the Alzette or in the Petrusse? Or in a cheap novelette? Certainly not! Who ever knows the Petrusse? This spat out rill between nowhere and everywhere. This cheap novelette of tears. The homecomers solid line of cars? It does not give a shit about the way of the world. People jammed into sheet metal have their own laws. Big Brother laws. Laws spat out. Laws spawned in spat screenplays. And the larger the mass of the jammed, the more insignificant the reason for jamming. And once he, the Terminator, sits in the passenger seat, the babbling starts. What? The story is cancelled. Shit, I'm too late! What should I do now? Fucking car! Fucking traffic jam! Fucking story! I hate this car. This life. This word! You cannot do this to me? You are the last asshole. You get the last word? No, the breakdown service does not help now. Neither does the thesaurus . That takes too long! Simply try to progress! Come up with something! Now go ahead! Call me a taxi then! No! I do not want to know about it. I do not care. That makes no sense

either! Do you know what time it is? Exactly! And they have announced this gigantic traffic jam on the radio. On the Adolphe Bridge? Of course! Where else? But you know full well that it always jams at this time on this stupid bridge! Of course I know that there are also such traffic jams on Brooklyn Bridge. What has that to do with it? Do you want to take the piss out of me? Yes, I am irritated! Yes, exactly. It is plugged. I say, the key is plugged. In the story. Of course you cannot see it. It has broken off! The other piece? What do you want with the other piece? That's not possible. Because it cannot work. No, it cannot. Is that my problem? Just for the hell of it. You are who? Terminator? I do not understand! Explain it to me later. Got to go on. Later? There is no later!
Too much ambiguity all at once makes no sense.
Hurray! Broken seconds.
Hurray! Broken nights.
Broken bridge pillars.
Broken sausages.
Broken people.
On the way home.
Broken destinies. Home matches.
Broken traffic jams.
Traffic jam breaker.
Traffic jam criminal.
Traffic jam slips.
There you are astonished! Promised time adjournments. Promised detours. Ways out. No walk in the park these days. Thick time floes float in the Alzette. But clod is not equal to clod. Time not equal

to time. If it is milky, the time was not quick enough. It does not control itself. Not itself. Not me. Perhaps you? Always too slow! Or too fast! Never in time. Never on the scene of the event. Never on time. Is too forgetful. Throws away its seconds. Like a compromising murder weapon. Like sinister thoughts. Needless ones. Helter-skelter thoughts. It is a raven time. A hoax. A vain breakdown announcement in the time traffic jam. A chaotic second in the rush-hour's traffic stress. The time of the world thrown on the Adolphe Bridge. The time-lapse in advance. The time gaper in the waiting loop. The slow motion in the looping. The time in the arse. I look trough the time window and lo and behold! It waves on more time with the time ticket. Scoop a trip through the troublemakers' life which prevents me from collapsing. Stuck in their daily traffic jam, they ram me. With their compassionate glances. Their haughty sniffs. The foot squeezed onto the shaky brake. The fingers wound around the stiff steering wheel. The yaps are swearing. The teeth stinking. The scrotums scratching. The arses sweating. The traffic jam starts boiling. The sausage is cracking. The nerves lie bare. Time dawdles away. Like skinny first lanes. To the left, people. To the right, people. The traffic lights dance rain dances. Oh no, not that! It is raining black time filaments. The Alzette swells. The time floes are melting down, blasé. Fading in final flotsam. Expelled, I'm killing time in one of these fucking cars which will cart us to the madhouse. Broken fingernails stick in clenched teeth. The day of reckoning approaches.

What have I done? I bleed the daylights out of me. All of it has a reason! To err is human. Feminine? Capricious? Dislikes being ignored. Remaining unobserved. Not taken. But what a diva: time. This bodes nothing good. What should it mean? That we do not flow to New York? The Alzette and I? All of it goes down the drain? All of it is lately going wrong. Only what's biting omen? Never did I have such a strong sense of time, such great willpower. I am absolutely convinced of my plans. My story. Will reach the chosen target. However, all of it reverses against me. You too! Do not be so hypocritical! You do not really want to get out of here. Out of this story. Help me! You are hurting me! Ouch! The sense certainly will stick out. It will surrender. Wait! A sec. Somebody will understand it. However ugly it may be. I see the river. Of time. Ahead of me. The story comes to life. The Alzette squeezes through my tear duct. And stinks like the howling misery which slinks through the bowels of the rush-hour wrong ones. Time sometime leaves marks of putrefaction. In me. I must lie down. I do not want to hear anything more, see anything more. No, leave me be. Please! Five minutes. Five seconds. No, I do not cry. You do not understand. I wished you would trust me! Back me. Didn't we once have the same dreams? No, I cannot imagine it either. But I can barely await it. Am hassled for no reason. The escape from the Alzette Valley is approaching. That's the way it has been happening for eternities. Total commitment on the willpower's service. Of poetry. Of modification. Of illusion. The strategy is obvious. Out of the mess. Out of the Adolphe of the bridge. Out of the traffic jam. Out of the story. Termination with Terminator. Termination with sense! The story without alpha and omega. The sausage of the sausages. Without center. Without meat. Endless futility. An egg dance of feelings. A refreshing chaos in the boredom of the sad system. Of the home-comers. An attempt! Hardly worth mentioning Nobody wants to admit his fear of futility. The world championship of the knotted words approaches. I'm working out hard. I am the future all-categories world champion. A glimmer of hope in the alphabet's desolate desert. Springer does not surrender. That was clear. Was bound to happen. It makes no sense to make sense. Be honest for once! One should peel off his fingernails separately! This would be the solution of the problems. That nobody asks. No more occupational therapies! What would the world look like without story? Without yesterday? Without tomorrow? Without evolution? Without purpose? For years a fingerless fighting. Without weapons. Without fight? Against a jamming in the getting on. In the reverse gear! Three jumps ahead, two aback. Genuine aggression in the progressing world cultural heritage. History on strike. In agitative panic. The sense hidden in the hunger for it. Stuck in the constant reverse gear. In the brand new home-comers's car. In the spick and span jam of the day. Not tellable in a normal way. But it will work out! Must clap! Clatter. Flutter. That's the way it's been lacking for an hour. The words stand amok. The words punch themselves in the wrong direction. Opposed. Thrown into a mess. The knots assume shape. Knot themselves twice and triply. Umbilical cord knots! Existence knots! Hunger knots! Hunger for freedom. In the most true sense of the words. Life's collar is bursting. Out of fashion mental resources get caught. Explaining the meaning is unnecessary. But in sequence! One at a time. The facts are collected. On digital rubbish dumps. The globe is a jam. A disc. A thin one! A digital one! A packed one! The knowledge, all of it jams. In a zero. In a one. We daily get gazillions of new inputs. From the traffic jam upon the Adolphe Bridge the first cries for help break through. Twin-towers of screams are collapsing. They fumble in deaf keyword swarms. Entire sentences swim amok. Like carcasses in the Alzette. They jump into absurd horror stories. Biographies. Tales. My life! My family! My God! The Alzette trilogy runs wild. City of hate! The shadows strike back! And Terminator gets stuck. In the window gap! The Alzette in the swarm of explanation. The traffic jam in need of explanation. In the regression. Of the story. That crumbles. And loses. Like the melting cube. In the pressed sugar. Of the sweet doom. Of the exhausted closing time. Of the stung words. You'd better take your trigger finger away! From this word. This row. Hello! Do you hear me? What's your intention? Nevertheless, you do not believe I would be in the mood. To sweet-talk to you? I do not feel like it. No more time! Since it does what it wants. Time! Has come. Tripped! Over piling up wordfalls. Untense excitement. Makes itself at home. Like a bloated motherfucker. Not like that! That's not the way it works. Conform to the rules, man! Do not try to play the peeper here. The Superspringer. There are rules! These rules are scuffproof. Timeless! The day is just swarming of irregular seconds. That have no place in it. Not on this day! Maybe on another one. Who can judge that. Every day is a sausage with two ends. A jam of seconds. A steal of seconds! Life a field butcher's shop. At full speed! God a head slaughterer. In a white smock. The battle knives are sharpened slogans. Fractions of seconds! A mess. One takes some of them and transplants them into the next day. Does it change history? Probably not. Does it split them? I prolong my arm and send them beyond the undulated hereafter. The smoothed seconds. Which rage in the storm of my head. Like the butcher knives of an enraged head slaughterer. Or even worse? Battle cries in the traffic jam! What is the trouble over there? Why does it not go on? I sit on two hundred strained horses and am not getting on! The horses snort and fart. Their foam of anger spits in the cowardly sundown. Shrill confusion of seconds in one of these ordinary burned days. That can be spent on the Adolphe Bridge like tiresome evenings. Passed days of stagnation. Wrong disconnections of seconds. Overestimations of time. Tongue strikes of swooning fury. Blows in the face. In the face of the story. In the story of the home-comers. The home-comers of the eternities. The eternities of the time frames. And all of this on one single ailing stone bridge. Stone! Time! Bridge! All of it fits. In the battle of my words. Spiked with friendly fire. The seconds vow vengeance. Terminator squeezes out of the window gap. Loses control. Coolness! All he is composed of. And the Alzette jumps out of bed into the nitty-gritty. Flooding in the belly. Tsunami feelings in the womb. The dams are too close to bursting point to have time for wonder. I wonderfully reach the beach of madness and dip my greedy hand in its desire. I am a writing debacle. With washed hands. In the blood of the massacred words. That are swelling. In the jam of my story. That becomes thicker bit by bit. Say, has it become thicker? At the beginning it had a beautiful belly. It was so slim. A gazelle. Did you invent that? Is that your story? There you are! Some of it was not good. Really not. Was it? But I must feel free, otherwise I cannot avoid myself. And neither can the seconds. Therefore! Just dare! Look at it! You eyewitness. You finger pointer. Look into my words. Look into the black. Of time's bull's eye. That has passed. That has gone. You early booker! Of the trip. Into the jam. Of the memories. The stubby ones. Of the stony bridge. Above the valley. Of the bestial elapse. Of time. Here's looking at you, kid! When you are laughing. With two blue-eyed knots in the face. Of the aging waves. In the speed mania. In the sea of the dimples. Trapped between two waves. Your smile is only a small sausage. In the mincer of the shabby expression. Of the feelings. Which are wringing themselves. In the jam of the deluge. Of the laughter. Foam which you make when you see how I slave away. At the attempt to radiate. In the collision of the atomic second beats. Which dart at me. Packed! Like at a time killer. A limitless one. Tasteless one. Whom the laws of elapsing time strangle. Who shifts their borders! Who gets over the anxiety! Who thinks lightly! Too lightly. Maybe! However, thinking alone is not enough! Especially not indeterminate thinking! Rule number 6: Float forward mercilessly! Oops! I get to the point. Exactly! If I only want, I am the best. If it were only always so! But no! My moods are exhausting. I believe the story falls bit by bit. Goes down. The skin! Of the bearable. All the same! Thus I do not reach New York! My dreams have a hard job! Today? No, always! I still intend to do so much. Leave me! I would like to cry! No, alone! The story is over! As if it wanted to escape from the jam, the Alzette of my spat-out story rises out of my boundless eyes and flows in panic into the horror of the looming morning. The valley's panaroma curve is bravely bending my look. It dawns. On me! There is no good reason for the overflow. Of details. Some people just want to be lied to. With true lies. True stories. For example: The sausage that I mean is the end of the world. Don't panic, I say! All's going to be fine. But it does not work out. It piles up. It's nearly torture. This cannot go on like this. It screams to high heaven. There you feel queasy. No more laughing matter there. There you go! I cannot even cry as I used to. Much less shout. Write! That's going too far. I must let go. If I want to fly, I must let go. But it does not work out. You cannot always stick to all of it. You are getting mad! How do you want to bring all of it under control. You never leave a bit out! If you were at least crying. Of course simply like that! Why not? That does not hurt. But you do not believe this yourself. Spiders do not cry? Which spiders? I spin? Lay off, will you! How are you talking to me! I'm even flying on alone. The words? Whose words? Mine? What should be wrong with these words? They are flying along, of course. Where? Somewhere. To New York, for example. Sure that is good. I know that myself. No, I did not try it yet. But still everybody can dive into the story. And it also has a sense. That you should know it the best of all. But you have experienced it! Yeah, just go! I still have to work. Rule number 1: Let go! Over and over again let go. If you want to let go, you must fly! But rather on your back! To the traffic jam. To the troublemakers. And do not look upwards! In the sky! The floating one. The sweating one. Fly above the Adolphe! Above the clouds! Above the jam! Otherwise you get sick. Sky sickness! Hard to heal. In the flying. Extremely dangerous! If you are once stuck in it, time rots your teeth off. The days and seconds. The remaining ones. The last ones. Then you are done. Finally! Let go! You must let go! You too! The Adolphe Bridge already curves down. Under the pressure. Of the charge. Of your past. That you leave behind. Throw away. Just for the fun of it. En passant! In the flyby. Abandoned. Thrown away. Without having processed it. Without having finished with it. Without having thought of it. Once skysick! Always skysick! A pest.

It rankles itself into your blood and leaves spoors in the genes. Overtaking spoors. Of air holes. Of solitude. Which are embarrassed. The results of the skysickness. Are strange solitudes. Brilliant ones! You will experience early enough what you could have had with me. If you had not taken me that seriously. Would not always interrupt me! At that time! From the outset! All of it too much? Your bad luck! You are never going to find a guy like me. You can bet your life on it. Me? Your poison? I am damn scratchy, but toxic? Well! Full of scratches! But whole! Minded. And solitude without scratches is an Adolphe Bridge without traffic jam. A sperm without ejaculation. A sleep without dream. An emptiness without purpose. A breakdown. Of the nerves. Without cooling. They overheat! Like tuned engines. At full speed. At standstill. Oh be quiet! What are you talking about? What do you know about it. I am the one who has the feeling. Time passes and nothing happens. I must experience something. Damn! The head slaughterers of the holy Alzette already brandish their weapons at me! But I am too young. To decay. Want to experience the world and be experienced. By the wondering troublemakers who are stuck in the traffic jam and welcome any change! Why not scratch? At the disc. Of the window. At the temper. At yours. At the facade. Of solitude. Through which you fly. Like one letting go. A loser. A squished Terminator. Like the crumbling bridge stones. The skysick people of the home returning dreams. However, just let me do it! This story is going to last at least till tomorrow. And please turn on the radio. I want to hear what's going on in the world. Whether the traffic jam has dissolved. Yet, you know that the story must be ready tonight for dinner! No, not ready for printing. You just have to read it out. In your deluxe apartment. Or was it in the travel agency? Or was it the itinerary which you wanted to check? Beyond the bridge. At the office. Towards New York? Yes exactly, where you want to go. Home? Call it as you want! For the time being you are stuck in the knot of the traffic jam like your scrotum hair in the zipper of your front seat passenger. Exactly! And Terminator obstructs the window gap. The emergency exit. The escape route. I see! Oops! Toady! There is no escape route. Listen to the TERMINAUTHOR! To the author of the fencing words. Or rather to that of the creeping ones? The slimy snail words? Then read in snail tempo! Snail stories! That creep away into their shell. Taken by the first word. Read on at the faintest suspicion of sense. And convulsed. With laughter. Buried laughter. In the secret corner of the slime. About the recognitions and other stories. Since something is always missing! The red sparrow! In this oracle night! Behind locked rooms! Freeze! The skysick people get stuck. The bridge flies above the bare backs of the home-comers. The story is over. Out of pity! Off with time which vanishes. With you! I have warned you! I have seen them! Wanted to save them. I have spoken to it. What do you say? You are not coming along? Why not? You are afraid? Listen to me! If you do not come along, the bridge will collapse. For sure! Exactly! If you step onto it, it's going to crumble away, that's for sure. You should listen to yourself! Well then simply fly over it! As you always say, you could do all of it if you only wanted to. So please! Want to! As if it was so easy to want. To speak to time. Its falsification. To the skysick ones. The troublemakers. The snails. The scratches. The gogos. Those letting go. The home-comers. The scrotum hairs. The Terminators. To the toadies. To the loneliness. To the Adolphe Bridges. The floating ones. Those flying past. Those moving. Those without a trace. The eyewitnesses. To the battles of words. Sabered ones. To the time flayers. The maniacs. Call it as you like! It ain't easy. Call it a story. A spell. A too thin one! It is too dull to only read the black. Touché! I understand something! Even the puny details between the lines. Hurray! Touché again! I am a hero. Get me out of here! I even understand something more! Understand what's printed. Squeeze the mind. I will put the fear of squeeze into the printed matter. Take matters into your poor fingers and express it. Crush it. Prod it off the edge of the book. Disgust it out of the story. Dispel it. Into the lines jam. The cells jam. Will finish the lines off! Knot them. Sausage them! Tousle them! Hurray! Once and for all! Finally! Offer the story an end. The end of a sausage! Of a pipsqueak. Write a mash for the story. A sausage meat. The words spell knots. Spell pigtails. Pubic hair curls. It would be altogether lacing the jammed thoughts. Unique! A bridge above time. In the wailing valley of the Alzette. This vein of desolation. In the jam of the head. Of the story. A limitless wish. A daily fight. In the almighty solitude! In which words could diffuse. Like laughter. In the face. Of freedom. Clean of story and sense. Of pinched words and sentences. Reflected thoughts and masterminded painfulnesses. Without story you are faceless. An integrally different person! You are talking, laughing, having fun. Is it there, in your eyes, it is as if you were not. As if you were only a background. Your face only the sheet on which it was written down. Your laughter wrinkles the scars of the skin in which it was scratched. Does it not bore you bit by bit? Somehow? I mean, I do not understand you! Different every time. Who are you finally? I don't even care. I have nothing to tell you. And have got used to you. Everything is OK! You are! I am! Boring? I know! Yes, this does not bother me. Sorry? Abandoned in the Alzette? It is only one miserable rivulet. An embarrassing mistake! A wet fart in the valley of the jammed Adolphe Bridge. Of the bloated one. The one gobbling up home-comers. You ought to know that. You should! It is only one part of the network. Of the sock. A little vein. In the blood clot of the horny waiting in a dull autoqueue. Of madness. My dear! The globe is a disc. And a jam. A jam disc. So what difference does a single day make? Screams the car radio! Upon the Adolphe Bridge. In Terminator's furtive hiding place. And promptly this one starts to blubber again! Always fond of jokes. The odd bird. This zero! This one! Loves it to overact. "I don't give a shit", he screams. "Get me out of here!", he whimpers. But I give shit about it. I give shit about me. Leave me in it! I am only the born spectator. I am not stuck in the jam of things. Of the bridge! Of life! Not yet! I am still filled with high spirits. Foolhardiness. Lust for life. Suspicion. Am stuck in a story which seems to become none. None which is to be read as such. And your jam is what I am sick and tired of. The moaning. The everlasting one. And even more the not moaned one. The accepted. The suffered one. Terminator in the gap. Of glassy time. Which is bursting into thousand splinters at the least pressure. The horses are rearing. The melting tarmac becomes engrossed in merciful thoughts. The crumbling bridge looks for recovery of damage. The accepted bridge name pities itself. The accepted brook name is unnecessary. The accepted front car guy pukes. To the enemy. To the red light. The accepted home-comers's crowd. To the crowds of expectants. These impassive long-term parkers. To these timeless time scalers. These thought through futures. Those who thought there would be something to think. In advance! Something that even they would understand. Something generally understandable. Mass compatible. Generally known. À gogo. And here they are again! The troublemakers. The strike breakers. The time criminals. Falsely written slips of the tongue. Always they come at the strategically right moment. From their point of view! When it is convenient to them. To them, not to me! Not to my stupid attempt to write no continuation. None for them. No useful one. No meaningful one. No devoted one. No necessary one. Not even possible one. Not absurd one. I do not not care! I drown these ideas. That's it! In the moaning of the Alzette. The plagiarism of the Petrusse! In me. In all haste. Since if not now, then when? When the jam has broken up? And how should this work out? There you go? Once doesn't count! Even if it dissolves now, tomorrow it's going to be there again. Rule number 14: A traffic jam never comes alone! Has allies. Secret lovers. Collectors. Observers. Jam erotics. Jam fanatics. Who would flip without the daily jam on the Adolphe Bridge. Or on the Brooklyn Bridge. All the same to me! Imagine them, the jams, crowded with freaked out fanatics waiting in vain for their daily dose! Taxi drivers with withdrawal symptoms. Missionless terminators. In quest of a mission. Stress-free home-comers. Whistling ones. Singing ones. Those writing dense poems. Complying with time. At home on time! That provoke artificial jams. To protract it. It, the usual waiting. The beloved one! The needful one. No waiting no life. No bumper to bumper traffic no lust for sex. No adrenaline. No pressure. No sperm. No excitement. No fun. No end in mind. The Adolphe Bridge as dead. Extinct! The Alzette valley wizened. The home-comers only shadows of their former selves. Silhouettes of a remembrance of better times. Times of prosperity. Times of unhoped-for encounters. And? Also stuck, Motherfucker? In the armoured jam? Bomb jam? Religion jam? In the sewage jam of the medieval world ideals? Jam friendships are those which do not break so fast. Getting the regular space in the daily jam! Booking jam spaces! Winning regular jam space fights! Addressing jam audiences! Jam babbling! Jam stammering! Jam simmering! A life without jam is a life without sense. Jam sense! Jam abstinence! So that our arrogant Terminator penetrates into the satellite navigation system and zaps the woman's balmy voice in the system. A tidy one. A declaration of love! A prediction! That is good to hear. Up to the point of the jam. Where he belts up her helpful mouth. "At the next crossroad turn to the right!" With tongue strikes! Which do not want to stop dissolving the jam. "In one hundred meters turn to the right!" As if there were this solution! As if the jam would melt in the saliva of a charming woman's voice. "In fifty meters turn to the right!" As if a radio-wave would be enough to solve the knots of the Adolphe Bridge. To release. To blow it up. With short-wavy kisses. Flooded, the system bubbles pointless ways out into the wide-open ears of the greedy home-comers. Seduced and woozy they listen to the voice struck. For seconds struck. "In twenty meters turn to the right ! Do now turn to the right! Jump!" She does not know any more what she is saying. She loses control. She is hallucinating! However, Terminator bites dutifully in the point of the digital tongue. And in the depth of twenty meters the bitten-to-pieces point of the sluggish Alzette flows leisurely as if all of it was normal. All of it under control! All of it fine! As if it had all the time of the world. Trapped in its syrupy bed. In its mud with the seconds soaked up. However, the voice keeps on talking. Despite a raging Terminator between its teeth. Purposefully chasing the home-comers into the abyss. Pitilessly! And they obey. Blindly! Hardly surprising! Navigation systems eat up heroes! Best on ways home. In traffic jams. At crossroads. At the next one it becomes silent. Digestion time! Long seconds. Exhausted predictions. Which do not pay anymore. The binary disc glows. The system melts. Terminator has worn it out. The woman's voice! It tosses around. Shrieks. Hops. Flattens the information. Trips! From one forecast to the next. The exits get caught up. The future is a slice. Of a salami. A jumpy one. A diversion jumping into the Alzette. Divergence! The disc of a sausage. A coldly cut one. And time rummages in these assorted cold cuts. Spouts out of the system's slit. Which does not recognize it. No more able to read it. Because the confused voice and the exhausted Terminator have messed things up. Have jumbled the exits. Confounded the detours. Thrown all of it down the brook. All of it! The Alzette. The Hudson River. The slit of the Adolphe Bridge. The slice of power. Of the system. It flies through the remaining cars and frightens the home-comers to hell. Not the Springer. The one crashed into the Alzette. The one not jumped. The non-Springer. The coward! The jam addicted. The seduced. The longing. The Adolphehooked one. Who, on the bridge, is waiting for the end of the world. Is adoring a slice. Only to put other ideas into his head. Any ideas at all. Ideas do not belong onto this slice of time. Not onto this page of the story. Since it does not stop leading us astray. Into detours which we do not want to adopt. Not at any price. Our jam is sacred for us. Our faltering is on purpose. We are the coward mercenaries of the waiting. We sacrifice ourselves. We are ready to die. For less than nothing. For the jam in the jam paradise. The Adolphe Bridge's one. Representative of all jams. Of all times! All home-comers! Ready to be accepted as coward heroes. In the kingdom of heaven of the jam heroes. Of the skysick slice-devourers. Long live the jam on heaven's bridge! Endless life! And on it goes! With endless time. The cowardly, not in the abyss jumping, second-accumulating one. With the time slice practice shooting. 5.16 pm! Time goes its way. Rule number 2: Never ask what time it is! It is too late for that! You should have asked earlier. Before the jam! Before the entry into the story. Of the bridges. Above the Alzettes. And even if the jam lasts for years, what difference does it make? Whether you despair? Get mad? Or keep cool. And for fun, tease the home-coming woman in the car behind you, who puts on more lipstick, and you impregnate her, just because she winks, and leave her, just because afterwards your scrotum itches and you then fall in love with her, just because she is the only woman in this goddamned jam who has reacted to your window knocking, just because she has flatly mistaken you for the Terminator, however, in retrospect it makes no difference to her who you are, just because she has always wished for children, but there was no question of love, that was not worth it, that was not the deal, that you should have considered earlier, now it is too late, never ask what time it is, these times are gone, the train has left the station and is stuck in another jam which can also last for years, so what is the point of the cellphone terror which you are staging, to at least talk with her, about what, I beg your pardon, in a jam the topics of conversation are quickly stumped, the sausage, you can see it in the rear-view mirror, both of them are fucking like jam rabbits, not the knots of the sausage, in which you are stuck like mangled lovesickness, no, I'm talking about your impregnated love coincidence, bottled with your grotesque jam sperm and the sperm sopping Terminator which squeezes into every slit which presents itself to him, to whom it meanwhile makes no difference which mission he has to accomplish, the main point is, he gets rid of his superfluous Terminator stuff, he who in the jam of the Adolphe Bridge does a doctorate in Sperminator, even if afterwards he is stuck in your window gap, like a wimp in your wanky mitts, just because out of hate you want to cut his throat, with your electronic window, which you press as if it were sausage or nothing, life, the schlock of time, in which you already hear your children in the car behind you screaming you to blazes, as if it was your guilt that the jam has got stuck and you are not the chosen one, for which this jam madam has mistaken you, a fuck long, and are yet the one, otherwise, it would never have come to this, although it is not going a meter further, since 5.16 pm, just because the big things in life are not measured in meters, especially not when you are making love, like an uptight bullet in the barrel of a rusted machine gun, although this would still be understandable in a jam, where the smallest advancement behaves like newly discovered galaxies. However! The jam on the Adolphe Bridge is an aberration. In the cracked universe! And several galaxies are but star-sniffing slices which smile at us extremely earthly. You run the risk of mistaking these heavenly grimaces for those of the head slaughterers. You know, when they sharpen the knives! Yes exactly, that's the smile I mean! They mistake us for rabbit lump droppings. Since the jam on the bridges of this world cannot look different. Just believe me. I have seen it. From far above. Have smelled it. From far away. The stench of the jams. Of the Alzettes in my own car. Because there is no ventilation in these situations. Never! No toilets. No movement. No progress. In the story. The time gets caught. Brags! Grumbles! Suddenly pretends to be standing still. Stand-still seconds in rank and file. Sky-high. In tense length. An optical illusion! If you are only deeply enough caught in the droppings of the rabbits. Instead of wasting your precious time in utopian lightning-speeds. Seconds commit crimes! Against me! Mainly against me. Since I have all the time in the world! To entertain these thoughts. These blurred ones. These useless ones. And that was about it again. All this seems very strange to me, nevertheless! Is a curious game. This clamping. This dribbling. This getting caught. In trifles. That troop. Lump together. Into a story. An insignificant one. Hushed. Tied up. For deaf people improper. Enchained seconds which rebel. Slave pearls which slave away. Sweaty time extensions which pursue each other. A captivating sausage meat. One cannot tell this at all. Seriously! One must shout this! I shout! Don't you hear it? Before the vocal chords knot. Because they are so cheeky. So combative. And before the shouts make sense. Which consists of nothing but small senseless sounds. Which fight together. To snatch an honorary place in the cacophony of this life. Which is in delay! Because it is stuck! On the bridge. In the jam. In the country of the immovable rivers. Of the deep silences. Hello! Is anybody there? You appease the depth of your home-coming thoughts with horrific close-ups of the elapsing time which stains your windshield. You switch on the windshield wiper. The thoughts smear. Your time! Each and every one bends under a wafer-thin recollection. Like under an unaffordable revelation. The days spent in the jam have lost too much time. The back of the experienced curves with the time. The flying one. It bends the determination of the bridge. Down! It sags. Like the overbred paunch of a pot-bellied pig. Which wallows in the time hole. Bequeathed by the jam. Of the sausage! A future hollow. The future sepulchre. Bridges are future pigs. Pigs are future sausages. Sausages have predictable ends. Ends are knots. Knots are future destinations. Destinations are future sepulchres. And pleased the jam grunts its pork dreams in the scenery of this story. Mine! And actually has no place there at all. Except the innocence! Of the words! These sausages of the letters. Which twirl around your thoughts like prison bars. And rather shut the fuck up. Not to be misunderstood. It could seal your fate. What was said. What was thought. Funny. Amusing. Retained. Repressed. Swallowed. Strangled. Taken word for word. The exceeded limits. The ridiculous rules. The dull styles. So that the gravity of the jam does not let you jump into the depth of the Alzette. You may laugh! The Alzette laughs at the Petrusse. Serves you right! I took the fight out of you. I become famous. I am a plagiarism. I am the biggest. And only because I sound better. And my blade cuts better. Into the meat of the home-comers. In the reading brain of an average story lover. A pedantic bookworm. Which leaves my ship as the first. That's only fair! Away with them! There's an end of beginning and end! Of the knots! Away with the average! Of the sausage. All of it is sausage! All of it is a slice! All of it plagiarism! All of it too regular and too well-behaved. The home-comers are. The jam causers. The jammed. The retarded are. And Terminator is. To each home-comer his Terminator. And the Alzette is. To each bridge its Alzette. And all of it is to. To too! Too closed. Too in itself. In dead-endlessness. In jams. In queues. In fictive autoqueues. In irritating cash desk queues. In bus queues. In cash dispenser queues. In employment agency queues. Confession queues. Waiting room queues. Letter queues. In queues which confuse. Drag enigmas. Like a veil. Exterminate secrets. Like nicotine addicts their fume. Dolorous retching. That forms a face. In itself distorted. A grimace which tells a story. A toxic one. Meandering one. A mass of its own laws. Of the rehearsed expressions. Namely the frightened twitching eyebrows. The shaky corners of the mouth. The knots of the sausage of the mouth. The luminous eyes. The knots. Of the sausage. Of the looks. Burning looks. Indignant head-shaking! Negating fending off! Not like this, my dear! Not with us! That's not the way you are going to creep on the quiet into OUR JAM! What are you in fact smug about? Who are you anyway? A Springer? What? A stand-by man? One jumping around the corners of reason? With which privilege? According to which rules do they jump here? Which sense should this make? None? Oh! You mean, sense is nonsense? Because you are what? A poet? Ha-ha, that's a laugh! Even for crabs. In the Alzette. And Terminator. Whipped into shape. In the window gap. Or between the legs of the lady behind you. And the horse powers of the stand-still autoengines. And the heartbeats of the home-comer's hearts threatening to stand still. Which do not get rid of the stress any more. Most assiduously amassed bonus points in stinky offices. Frustrating harassment attacks of unknown enviers in superior number. These snipers of a global world. This is very important to it. To this world! This fight! For the best places. In the jam of things. Of the sentences. Bumper to bumper. Sentence to sentence! Which do not progress. Want to! May! Should! But the time of the dense words remains! Is a bridge! Between the knot of monotony and that of the fast lane. Minimum time into hope. Full throttle into desire. Blind into danger of the unknown. Just like that! For fun! Jackass of impatience. Of poetry. It's in my hands. On the fingertips. The fingernails break off. Rammed into the keys. Like abutments into the belly of the impossible desire for sublimation. So that the stiff monotony beats it. All over! From the metal avalanches. And the literal fairy tales. Of a brave better world. But still I am lagging behind! In this race. I must be quicker! But speed is just one thing. However, the orientation is something else. I must raise the tempo. Accelerate! Sublimate! But is that the acceleration which I need? That you brave? There is no acceleration in the jam. From zero to one in no time? Sublimation cut in slices? It too a sausage? An illustrated illusion? It too with two ugly knots? It too only a desperate accumulation of hope? All the same! I have it down pat. What's the point? Only a few empty slices remain to me. Should this here become the immense sensation? But over there are a few more to come. Thoughts! Home-comers! Sentences! Columns of cars! Bad luck! I put the best sentences into order. Are they even able to reach the medals tables? Get me out of here! I get crushed! Potpourri! Tohubohu! Smog alarm! Slicy sheesh! The gold medal is the hub of the world. World champion of the knots! And my pretension is also another. No medal over one hundred pages sprint! In NINEPOINTNINE SECONDS! If I do not make it! To be convincing! The best are wanted! Although the finger movements already betray it. That it is so lala what this story becomes. The words are schlepping along. Are tapping on the wrong letters. The keyboard went crazy to the left. The senses surrender. To destiny! And you are present live. From new-German view. However, stay tuned! The show goes on! Time is stripping. Its crisp moon already peeps above the gristly navel. The desired view of her vulva is only a matter of seconds. Stay with it! From the umbilical cord cut winner to the skysick loser there are only millimeters. In the jam on the Adolphe Bridge one millimeter has to be equated with a wasteful light year. One which can not be caught up! Especially not with my modest means. The race is brutal. Fingernail-hard! Ladies and gentlemen! Jam erotics of all bridges! Unify! Times are hard! And dangerous! I breathe a puff of sublimated atmosphere in the tension's hollow of the Adolphe Bridge. It is a pot-bellied pig. A pressured-to-perform pig. Almost like in the past! One does not see them properly. These hollows! These are glacier fissures. Man-eating and carcass-vomiting ones! It is regarded as imperative to recognize the danger on time. With a liftoff into the edge forwards. Bridge travellers anticipate nothing of the jamming danger. The most important thing is discipline, otherwise you perish. Many have talent! However, stopping has to be managed. Random words! Nothing but dumb freezers. Animality roaring! In the desert. Of the defeated bridges! Hours! They enjoy great popularity. Since, in the end, these are my rules which roar here! It is my story! My bridge! My jam! Are my blows! On the weird fingers. Into the stunned faces. Which are grimacing either way. Thus

I decide how it goes on here. Or does not go on. How it capers here. Catapults. Capitulates. Savvy! That's how it is! On the flipped-open bridges of my freedom. Of my rolling Alzette. Of my river. My nowhither. And this with a determination which overwrites all ideas of a common home-comer by light years. Easily! So! All over again. Back to the beginning. All of it! Too much. All of it! Too far. The time! It elapses. Too fast! The sky sheds its hair in tufts. It's raining home-coming atmosphere onto the windshields. 5.07 pm. The wind is a slice too! The weather forecasts are definitive. No redeployment of the depression above the Cologne Bay. The nerves of the home-comers are stressed. On edge. Jam announcements à gogo! The jam on the Adolphe Bridge stretches out to Brooklyn. The Hudson River seethes in the heads of the commuters. The crowds give the waste of time a good lesson. They carry it off well. Are keeping cool. Respect! Wrongly, as it will turn out to be. All is over and done. Forward? Backward? The cities stand still. The rivers lump. Life is paralysed. It is over. Lovers are stuck in their women. The scrotum hairs in the zippers. The distant looks in the horizons. The satellites in the ozone holes. The oil tankers in the seas. The airplanes in the holding patterns. The spoken words in the television waves. The hopes in the one who died recently. The sausages in greedy necks. The fired chemical weapons in the melting skin particles. The earth in the Catch-22 situation. The future in the delay. The presciences in the predictions. The mud up to their neck in it. The pictures of the day in the satellite dishes. The substitute kidneys, the ova, the sperm, the fresh vegetables, the cows and pigs, in short, the sausage, the end, of the world in the deepfreeze-storages. Art in the sleazy hands of rutting curators. Music in forbidden pirate copies. The expressions in fossilized mugs. The shaven girls in slave-trader hands, the kidnapped children in impregnable cellar fortresses. The tiring sentences in ghost-written books. The terrorists in American presidents. The suicide bombers in paradises ripped apart, hope in the condoms. However, enough of it! The knots are bursting! 5.25 pm. Rule number 11: The position is what is important! Which space you take, in the jam! Where you are stuck! In the front? At the back? In the middle? On the fast lane? On the shoulder? You sit in your Mercedes and change bit by bit. With time! Into a hopeless straw which becomes the last one. One like me! I am your mutation! Put myself. In your position! After some hours it becomes too stupid to me. Hey! Understand me! I must just go over there. On the other side. Of the bridge. And transform myself into a Terminator who is stuck in your window gap and calls for help. Whereby he only wanted to help you. To corrupt your future. And while I got stuck in the sentence about this bridge which I wanted to make on the quick, you change pitilessly! Into a flatterer. A toady. Just come in! Sit down! Where do you want to go? I am going to New York. It's going to be a long trip. I know the jam like the back of my hand. I stand daily in it. Am a professional home-comer. No, it won't last much longer, believe me! It will soon break up. It always breaks up! What? You just want to get across the bridge? Why do you not walk then? Because you are afraid? No, the bridge has never broken apart! What bullshit are you talking? This is my car and here I determine the world! Who must go, who may stay. Please, you can stay! Entertain me! Tell me a story, but don't talk rubbish! Otherwise, I go berserk. If I know whom? Terminator! You mean the TERMINATOR? The killer from the future? Listen, what do you take me for, of course I know him! And I also know the rescuer of the future. Ha-ha! He sits next to me! Hey, I recognized you immediately. You cannot fool me. I have seen through you. And the fact that this jam lasts so long, is not normal either. All of this is only a trick! I am not that stupid! I understand, man! No Terminator is going to get in here. I have my tricks. Am not quite a back number. Do you think I am standing for fun on this stupid Adolphe Bridge? Just think! Why I should close the window? Not even a Terminator's fart fits into this gap. Now calm down! And after some pitiless hours you are going to change. For hours the sun has been ready to set. For hours the horse powers have been ticking over in the engines. The windshield wipers wipe the depths of the Cologne Bay into the Alzette. The women in the rear-view mirrors disguise themselves. The tires melt into an oil slick. The bridge becomes a padded cell. The tire-mash creeps over the bumpers. The passenger-seat windows open a bit. Swarms of terminators circle like ravens above the treetops of the Alzette Valley which gets deeply frightened in its abyss. The mood gets closer and closer to a slice. The tension between zero and solitude transforms you phrase by phrase into the wave of a queue. Into the dream woman of a werewolf. Into the resistance fighter of a home-comer's brotherhood. Into a happy sadist, a conceited punk, a remote-controlled cop, a subliminal literary critic, a perverted curator, a convinced jam expert, a religious fanatic, a failing autocarburetor. Into all pictures which you recognize in my dismayed eyes. I am shaken! I cannot believe it! So you know? About me? About the Terminator? You know the denouement of the story? I know about the length of every single of your scrotum hairs. Every vale of tears of your laugh wrinkles. Every wave of the predictable tides of your cerebral cortex. This greasy dustbin, which flattens under my very eyes. Into a slice the size of a football field. You are anybody! You are all of them! All of them who are stuck together with us in the jam. All of them who squeeze into it. Although it threatens to burst. And swells. Like a fat tick. Smeared in blood and desperate we search for a way out. In the rear-view mirror! In fictitious music dreams. In braggart weather forecasts. In bygone news. In arrogant events. As if one could dive into the past. Like with one's finger into the wetness of a woman. Like with the butcher's knife into the tender brain. This extinct star in your head. You are all those who seem to have all time in the world. All of them who hang on the nipples of patience like on the mother's milk of the real deal. All of them who are capable of metamorphosis.

Capable of all of it. Being all of it. Being able to be all of it. No fucking matter, what or who. When or where! Essentially stuck in the middle of it. The wetness. The brain mass. The jam. On the bridge. In another time. Another story. All of them comedians. All actors. All of it false. A slice. Of the sausage. A chapter. Of the story. A home-comer. Of humanity! A sausage meat. A hodge-podge. A mash of rubbish. Where are the hard bats of life? Where is the juicy steak? The nutritious? The must-have? Should I croak here? Rot? In the common grave of the small sausage eaters? In the jam of the cannibals? In the weather forecasts of the soul devourers? In the overticking engines of the nature devourers? Tell me! Speak! Answer! Do I say. And he! Hey, hey, relax, man! What's wrong with you? Are you the chosen one, or what? Never been trapped in a jam yet? It makes no sense to get excited like that. Such a jam has its own rules. There you must absolutely keep your head, otherwise you flip. Make no mistake! You cannot afford this. There is no gold medal for it. For freaking out. Rather just open the window one small gap! There is someone knocking. A lunatic. A jam rebel. Am I possibly an open window for the world? Terminator? Man, stop with this story! This makes no sense. What does he want? Ask what he wants! All of them they want something. He says. Angrily. And I answer! I say that he is imposing himself. Yes, he violates my story. Yes! You have no idea. You are only an ordinary home-comer. However, he behaves as if he had to give her a direction. As if to be stuck in the jam had a direction. If I am stuck I give a shit in which direction. The bridge is open in all directions. The knots at the end of the world are only hallucinations. Digital will-o'-the-wisps. Sedation knots. And the Alzette behaves likewise. Waggles with its tail as if there was something to waggle with. As if all of it was going greasily fine. The sausage. In butter. A tidbit. Of destiny. It splashes. The windshield is full of fat splashes. Future pearls. In the story. Every pearl a sentence to suspend. Above the rear-view mirror. Where the lady of the car behind is sending kisses in vain. Holding her impregnated belly upwards and sending sentences in braille that nobody understands. Another story! Time is a damn good liar. 5.57 pm. But what day is this? The day after tomorrow? Have months already gone by? Years? Whole lives? Complete stories? Even Terminator is no longer the same. Gray hair. Decayed teeth. Weak-willed! Has forgotten his mission. Saving the future? Killing the chosen one? Fucking the lady in the car behind? Catching the home-comer at metamorphosing. Dying! Stopping! To terminate. He can imagine nothing more. The car parade is relentless. There is no more compact oblivion. The jam is all of it! Only all of it! No more speeding. No departure. No choice. No option for decisions. No fair conditions. It does not go further! This endures furthermore. The shoulder a single battlefield. Of the decaying thoughts. A barrier to be expected. Before the end. In front of the crumbling wall. The pavements have the advantage of the last stones. I do not know what that should signify. The stones fall! Deeply! The Alzette becomes the Adolphe Bridge. The stones become water. However, the jam remains. Like an ant bridge it hangs above the broken-down vale of tears of the Alzette. Firmly knotted at the ends of this former bridge. Between the low and the high tide of the troublemakers in my story. Which is a distance! From the said. Which should tell nothing! Words make too many rules! Sentences make too many prisoners! The sentences of the bridge stones make leaps into the depths of the senses! And once the stones have fallen, the troublemakers will follow them. Sometime! After all I am sitting next to the home-comer par excellence! And am swallowing patience in inconceivable quantities. It cannot happen free of charge! There must be a sense behind this nonsense. Is Terminator chasing after me or not? Am I the one? The chosen one? Who should poke into the anthill of the aligned creepers? Who gave me this mission? An ant-head slaughterer? A troublemaker's troublemaker? The fear of collapsing bridges? In particular overcrowded ones. Which I must cross. Over there to the travel agency. A traffic knot between Alzette and Hudson River? Because there must always be some destination? My story too is a mission. If I fail! A quite clear one! However, I cannot tell it. Or want to! This would be dull. Like a thrilling story with a happy ending. But please! Not in my back yard! You can get someone else for it! There are already enough of those. Look at my hands before you spit into my face! Smile if you understand nothing! That's the way it works. Or do I look like a storyteller? A bridge builder? Like a stuttering Schwarzenegger? Application is all that counts! A sentence of mine and on it goes! This trip is not bookable. Early booker unwanted! I have the right to remain silent. And you more than ever! Remain silent! Wonderful, this silence! How you jump concentrically into my sentences. With your fleeing looks. Which do not want to admit. The fact that there is such a thing. Is permitted! Now the nerves play a role of course. Who stands it longest? You or I? I grant it to you. Really! But my lead becomes bigger. I am too quick! Especially in the freeze-up my thoughts move like speedy ant legs on the transformed Adolphe Bridge. Now that it is alive. It really exists. It shakes! It waggles! It swings! Like a laughing beer belly. An ejaculating dick. Puke gobbet! Spits tones in the beat of the struggling ant legs. So that I must keep my ears shut. This I must not listen to! And I must go over there. Just over there! Am cramming two bundles of screaming ant lumps into my ears and advancing one foot at a time. Advancing! Deciding! Targetting! The direction defines itself all alone. Do not break my sentences! I start to move. Struggle! Ramming sentences! Punching! Come what may! One ant after the other is screaming for help. Home-comer's ants in the death-struggle! A sweat cabin of nose-picking home-comers. An anthill of swearing drivers. Who dream of nymphomaniac women. Of foaming beer. A crumbling of steaming bridge stones. Which dream of comet's dust. A waggling of dreaming waterdrops.

Which dream of the sea. Bundled up. Knots of exciting bridging. Which lead to nothing. Me not to my purpose. Over there is recognisable. Targeting! Locating! On the other side I must arrive. Only there and nowhere else! But I trip like a bouncing pinball over the jammed bumpers of my burst sentences. Sentences like bounced dreams! Dreams of the page change. Of the river change. Of bridge change. Of the fear change. I have dared go outside, have put my foot out the door, have seen the fear of the bridge, have recognized the traffic jam, plunged into it, hammered with the fingers, broken off the fingernails, made the stones crumble, enticed the prickle of all anthills of the world into the arses of the home-comers, just like that, without compunction, forced them to the sweating out of their patience. Out of the tears of a saviour! So that everyone understands the cruel trip across the Alzette! Can book. Misplace and transfer it. Like a bad lover. A badgered story. A dazzling jam report. A lied legend! So that everyone understands the weather forecast of the dissolving depression above the Cologne Bay. Of the cheer for the Alzette. The plan is simple! Disentangling! The motives are numerous. And still! Behind the scenery of the jam the concealed gloating spreads. On the Adolphe Bridge. Cries for help! Exclamations! Over! It is all over! Hey Termy! Wimp! Where are you? Help me! I must get over there. Otherwise it is over! Too late! My time runs away! Is there anything worse than delay? But the rules are the rules. 6 pm! This is too precise a point in time. A heaven-sent opportunity.

Time of early booking has passed by. OVER! How could this only happen to me? How could this point only pass by so inexorably? This point is a stupid sausage spread. The early home-comers rush into the prickle of their arses. Finally! New York sweatily misses the long distance. Nearby, however, Termy knocks at the windshield and screams: "It is breaking up! It is breaking up!" Should this be a threat? An image of violence? After the fight of sentences the fight of images? You do not recognize the connection? Pathetic! Make an effort! Show me what is holy to you! To take a masters in jam business? To be a random interviewee of Channel Alzette? To recognize connections? I give you ALL THE TIME IN THE WORLD! Wouldn't you have thought me capable of that? You think I am a spinner? A spritzer? A springer? And that's just how it is! I spin! Net knots in the connections of the blasé rivers and clinched bridges. Sprinkle promising sentences of the horror upon the home returning troublemakers. Spray my insignificance. Jump abysses in the art of the narrative. Unstoppable rifts into this story. And who should hinder me? Termy? This ageing, cowardly actor? Who does not understand his script? Cannot read it? Who pretends to be the non plus ultra of the lifesavers? Nemo propheta in patria! Not on my watch! I cannot be saved! I am no jumping jack. No one to be released! No home-comer. No jam-affected one! No-one stuck in the muck! Although? Humph! Oh well! Who can claim that about himself? Karl? Clear! A spinner! A splash! A jumper! A braggart! A lecher! A sentence desecrator! A stories defier! A smirky one! Motionless one! One standing still! Licentious one! One without any trouble! An unimaginative one! Pitiless! Harmless! Not beginning! Halt! Stop! Slowly! You know meanwhile how it goes on. Once I get started. Once I start to blow up the jam. That of the words. Of the ants. Of the empty statements. Of the non-binding sentences. I connect them. Knit them together. The ant legs. Dam and pinch, inch by inch. Suck the letters out of them one by one. Out of pity! For fun and yawning boredom! About the severity of the stories. That one hears! Above which I drag them. These sentences! These legs! Like a colored rainbow. This is better for the thrill! Of my stem cells. And the good mood! Of my most sophisticated fears. If the permanently jammed, the eternally dammed started to freak out. Their tins. Their anthills. To exit! And to speculate on the causes. Nevertheless, there must be a specific reason for the daily jam? Some idiot has made a mistake? Some troublemaker has troubled the troublemakers? Some coward has braked too early? A freak has mutated into a home-comer and has squashed himself under a home-comer's car? What a debacle! A disaster! A piece of news. A daily prediction. A global jam cause. Or some captor has kidnapped Termy! Terminator has once again fetched up unfavourably on earth. Stark naked and in the middle of a bridging fast lane or a shaky crosswalk. In front of the feet of an imported kidnapper. Rescuers are clumsy fellows! Selected cowards. Captors. Time dispersers. The Adolphe Bridge comes up with quite a lot to keep the jam stayers in a good mood. The mass of the jam stayers on a bridge without jam! Fancy that! That would be bad! Worse than frustrated hooligans in the frenzy of a lost home match. That's what probably happened. But that cut him to the quick. The kidnapper. His arteries. The fact that he has caught the Terminator. Who has no mercy. And has cut him into slices. Snip! Snap! And now he knocks at my front seat passenger's window and blubbers. "I am so sorry! I did not want to cause a jam. I meant no harm by it. He wanted to tie me up. I cannot be tied up! I am the saviour of the world!" And I think, this way, my trip around the world is not going to work out. This way, I won't get to the travel agency. A bad beginning of the week. 6 pm. Standstill! This way I do not experience what I have in mind. My story is horrified! Crowds of naked beauties who dart brainlessly toward me take to their heels. The streets of New York honk by my nerve fibres. Brooklyn kissing me trips over my fingers. Which are holding a winning time ticket into Terminator's scared face. Hello! It's me! Have won first prize, you perfect idiot! I am the winner of a trip to New York. I must redeem the ticket. Even today! What time is it now? What? And you spit your tears into my ears! Leave me, I must go! I must get out of here. Must go over there. Yet, somehow I will get across this stupid bridge. That cannot be so difficult. I should what? Fly? Hey, you Motherfucker! Past history? Tail wind? We already had this. Do not give me that flying on the back and such nonsense, okay? I am the chosen one! The destined one! And stuck like a black pudding! Go ahead and take a slice of my skill! That of getting across. Of undoing knots. Anyhow I will get across. At all knots! The story is not over yet! This sausage is not eaten yet. The Alzette not in the sea. In the greasy, oil-refuelled one. The bridge has not crossed. My mind. Yours. Wait and see. Nothing better crosses yours neither! Except darning ants into your ears. Because of the moanings. Except affecting my advancement with your emotional fluctuations. Because I am the boss? It is no fun to poke into your howling. In the midst of patient home-comers who have nothing better to do than to analyze weather forecasts and traffic jam reports. As if there was a gold medal for it. For the best listening. For the best reproduction of the most insignificant news from yesterday. The depression above the Cologne Bay! The sky's flowing hair loss! The clouds's splintering breaks. The raindrops' tormenting hammering. Onto the patience of the bridge stones. Onto the tension of the ant legs. As onto a keypad at their mercy. A story worn by time. Rhythmical mind crossing. There comes a point where it is enough! The stones capitulate. The home-comers vomit. The horse powers trample themselves. Gallop right away. Steaming exhaust pipes in their nostrils. It does not stet! On our nerves! Dead end! A shutdown for life! Time gulping for the headway. Joking way. Further standway! All of it becomes too much! Is it! Already! Was not meant to be! Is rotten time! Is all the same sausage to me! Never mind! Is released to shoot. You think! However, that's not the way it works! The sun is to blame. Already almost set. The home-comers are to blame. For the drowning. In their patient sweat. New York is to blame. Only a slice of dream. An apple strudel. A burst one! The stench of the sluggish Alzette is to blame. The jam predictions are to blame. The person in front of the person behind is to blame. I am to blame! All of it is to blame. Not really! Nothing is really! No explanation makes sense. No solving. No enigma. Neither here nor there. There is to blame! The back is to blame. Flown on the back it does not become better. But, at least! Your day may come. At all costs. Forget the past! The jam ends behind and before you. These times are gone! One may not exaggerate time. Not take the fast lanes so dead seriously. It is over! The bridges are over. Do not over-span! Not cross them! Signifying is over. The overtaking. The narrative. The chapters. The story. It is not sufficient. Is not enough. The hot phase of the disentanglement begins. The decision approaches. Victory or defeat? Remaining stuck? Getting out? Coming across? Standstill? It is not in the stars. Not in the bibles. It stands in the traffic jam. It stands here. Written! As thought. Hammered. Rule number 18: Write it as you think it! Think it as you experience it. Hit it! Suck it! Like that and not differently. Stamp unbelievable images on the way. Home! Over there! Emotional tail wind. Flying escape. Into the uncertain. Dismember it! As it dismembers you. As it makes you an elementary particle. In a heap of mud. In standby position. In trailing restlessness. A stack of slices. The mess of a sausage. Cold cuts of congested meanings. Of excessive senses! How to maintain the motivation? If nothing is to be done. If all of it runs smoothly. All of it stands? All of it falters? You get the illusionary feeling that all of it is all right on earth. Hurray! Terminator blubbers. Hurray! The horses are burning. The hoofs stinking. Hurray! You survive the flowing-off of the Alzette. Hurray! The lebensraum extends onto your jam. Hurray! The lady in the car behind gives you a blow job. In the rear-view mirror. Hurray! You have a purpose. Hurray! You are a slice. Hurray! In the slit! In the moist one! Of time! Which gives you a blow job too. A redemptive one! You have the profile of the ideal saviour. Hurray! You smack Termy. Hurray! Stick your blown soul like a foxtail to the antenna of your weather forecasts. Hurray! Man, are you great! And you get out of the home-comer's car again. Hurray! You bloat yourself. You see the ants coming. Hurray! Out of your blown soul. They dart for the defenceless standstill. Of your dreams! Which have crawled away into the bridge stones. Eternally the stars make dust. Eternally the heroes creep away. Eternally the souls are blowing. For the fight. You see how it eats up the Adolphe Bridge dust particle by dust particle. Hurray! IT devours YOU. It chains itself to itself. It creeps into your car queue. It exterminates the home-comers. It curtails the story. It sucks its patience. Darkens the general image. Of the lady. In the rear-view mirror. Hurray! You are only a word bubble. SERRATE! AWAIT! CHOKE! HISS!

But you will make it. You are the epicenter of the universe. The missing elementary particle. The forgotten one! In an isolated corner. In a small galaxy. A valley. A miserable one. Through which a river tries to flow. Above which a bridge acts as if it was connecting something. Knots? Chains? Worlds? And you spit your tormented face onto this bridge. As you like! It is a dreamlike jam. A daily disaster. That pretends to be something special. A swaggerer! A braggart. Like you! A common exceptional jam. A sentence jam. Like you! Welcome to Alzette Valley! Hurray! You can do it! You will come across. This will become a big night in the story of the connections. Of the knots. A basic episode. In the matter of extremities. Excrements. Excesses. Ex-wives. Ex-bridges. Ex-sausages. Yes, the day of the empty bridges will come. Of the empty towns. Ex-New York exercises dry! Standstill bridges dream bored dust-looks above the dried rivers, and the parched seas drink the greedy rivers of time. Drained home-comers rush into the reflection of Ex-Terminators's tears. What is to become of this? Reflex-like, I blink in the rear-view mirror. Who disturbs my future? I can not believe it! Am squeezing out of this home-comer's car, do not know whether I am still inside or already outside, there I feel this humid smile on my breast. Am stuck in the window gap which I have opened myself. Am on the run! Frontally, Termy tears on me like a lollipop, in my back this stupid home-comer digs into my balls and from below this winking lady snogs my scant breast hair. What is to become of this? The cars start to honk. The tyres explode. The horse powers kick buckingly. The ants bolt. The radio stations send uninterrupted weather forecasts. The offices at the other end of the bridge are noisily shutting the doors. So that I exactly hear it! I become aware of it. Of nothing! That will become. Of my trip. Of my lot. All of it gambled away? The bridge stones crackle like crushed ant legs. Are playing with their life. Adolphe retreats ashamed into the legs of his wife, the bridge pillars. The Alzette splashes like the shits through the town. Adolphe jumps headlong into it. The Hudson River watches it via satellite. Live! And jumps after it. I am torn apart. Live! On stage! In the universe! And have trouble keeping my parts in cohesion. The window pane splits me. The lady flashes me. I am too quick! For this world. Termy splits me. In slices. For these sausage eaters. I become death's target. The home-comer swallows the wrong way. On my scrotum hairs. Which are dancing like ant legs. However, the ants help me. They are the black foot-steps. In the snow of this story! Tenacious stuff, these beasts. If you roll them as cuts onto your body. Black as the night! Which glimmers one sign-off picture after the other. Into the canvas of my sadness. Which has no more smooth spots. Black! White! Black! White! Hop! Hiss! Incessantly. I cannot watch it. Not listen to it any more. It kills the nerve! Torments. It has to mean something! To me? And I do not know where else to look at. Always just working hard. Watching. Listening. Participating. Commiserating. Understanding! What is there to understand? An inhibited jam? A dead end in nirvana? The scrotum hair in the addicted tongue of a home-comer? Who are all similar. All of them get off. All! Of them! Thick! Thin! Dumb! Dull! Are glimmering among the endless stream of traffic. Their shoes stick together in the molten caoutchouc. They start to teeter. Like monkeys in the zoo. Patiently. Empty. But do not topple. Home-comers never topple! Just because. They smile. Always! In expectation of the newest state of affairs. “This is an important announcement! To all drivers! The Adolphe Bridge is closed! The Alzette has joined the enemy. The sky is closed. The night is the hallucination of a glimmer. The stars are dusty remainders. The universe is a box camp. The last jam announcement a betrayer. Leave your car immediately! I repeat: Leave your car immediately! There is danger of collapse! Do you love your car? Your life? Then leave it! Leave your car and proceed in one of the other directions! This bridge does not end. And keep calm! Patience! We have all of it under control!“ The ants tremble in my scars. Clap their hands. Here we go! An autoqueue of ants clapping on your windshield is something terrible. A crowd dashing against your slice of thoughts is something hideous. Rule number 3: Never mind! Mind clapping thoughts! Cut them into slices. You don’t care! Should they! You still have windshield wipers! So go ahead and cry! Why not? Are stuck in the jam. Have no other choice. Are in the Catch-22 situation. I have already been waiting for months for it to break down.

I am prepared! Not with me. I am the chosen one! What should I care about it? I am on the way to New York. To the universe. Am not Terminator. Should he save all of them! Of course! Some will be astonished! Some come out badly. Off the jam. Off the nothingness. Off the mix-up which surrounds us, the climax of nonsense, the screenplay of the endless unhistoricalness. Eh? What should this become? Rubbish? Ant scars? Windshield wiper scratches? Tear dust? A false appraisal of the situation? Of the stones? Of the crumbling? A complete lack of understanding of the rules? An absolute violation of the warnings? A misleading resemblance with the dreams of a jam announcer? Of an unauthorised dream announcer? Of an I? Of a you? Miles of falling stars in sight! Dreams? A sausage connecting us? A reckless one? We? Knots in distress? Bavarian veal sausaged! No notion of nothing! Exiled to the limits of the sausage meat by the sacrosanct head slaughterers? Crushed inside. Outwardly unstuck. Cool! Cover! Greasy! Patiently waiting. For it to become unstuck. From us! The jam! And our hero. Home-comer? Distances himself clearly! From our purposes. Homesickness? Decides! Between Alzette and Hudson River. But anyway! You know about it. This feeling! Black! White! Black! White! Black! White! Loose contacts of the elementary particles. Chill of death desire. Devouring of the contortionists. Intolerable waiting. Pitiless kidnapping. The only mistake! Understanding too early! Writing sweat! It is so hard. Let us wait! Day by day! Where should this lead to? Since today I am involuntarily I myself. Let me finish speaking! I have nothing to change. About these off-sentences! The reason why I survive here should be delivered here. Clipping onto single signs of life! Today it is my task to inform the world that I am indeed caught, however still alive. It is important not to break off contact. To all hostages in this country: Hang on! Persevere! All of it has an end! Symbolic meanings? Dead loss! Unreal worlds. Shadows of ourselves! All those about to die are greeting you. I am speaking to you! Should all of us be condemned to decay in the woods of the Adolphe Bridge. Moments of life, lost for good. Ever since I can think the Adolphe Bridge has defined the life of my cells. A deluxe prison. The home-comers are the child-soldiers of the Alzette. Uganda flows through the bloodstreams of its hands. 6 pm: Mercedes-star-war! Powerlessness. No place to get rid of one's garbage. Maybe we are being shackled so that we eat our shit? Is all the same sausage. Without knots! What is it all about? Drinking the sun? Dada? Should a new game be begun? Is it the end of my dream? All of it too much? Too far! Thought? The ends incompatible? We are stuck in a difficult phase of our relationship. Do you notice it? Fear is only a bad nightmare. OOPS! Who are you? For just reading me? What do you presume? The same as I do? Rightly so! Paint it red! War should reign! Let me tell you. War! Because I firmly believe that you are the stealthy home-comer who operates the electronic window lifter and torments me in your window gap, about to tear off my balls. Bowel-war. Sausage meat war. No wonder that I discharge a last time! Lately many a time! Get rid of the whole stuff! Am not able to carry it with me for ever and ever. Like you your potbelly and your fabricated fairy tales. What? You have none? All the same! If I spritz, I spritz! There is no doubt about that! The point is not to keep the form. To correspond to the rules. To drone a story. Others may do this. I am not sausaged out of this mash. I take the liberty of all of it. Since all of it takes it with me. And am slipping in the puddle of the ground which gets lost under me. Like the civilized earth in the voluminous shoulders. Which knot themselves together! Nevertheless, would be a joke if I did not succeed to get unstuck of them. My strength is not further breakable. Tear my beloved scrotum hairs out of the home-comer's slimy mouth. Stick them again onto my hopeful scrotum which dangles in a carnival costume from me. Not before having shaken off the ticklish ant legs which were an amusing scrotum hair substitute. Squeeze a plausible marriage proposal into the bottom crack of the unstoppable lady from behind with the hopeful glances or between the eye slits, if you'd prefer this, and with ant help I sew Terminator's crying robot rescuer arms to my endless trunk. Which drips along. Which he does not like, Termy, of course. But why should I bother my scatterbrained head about the destiny of someone I did not summon, as I am busy enough to squeeze out of the jam of painful things? In the end, all of it remains, as usual! Old fashioned! And I am busy.

Have a ticket! Have to cash it! Otherwise it is too late! It is always too late! The legal process is excluded. The situation delicate. The sense of all of it slides into the endless. All of the end, so to speak the knot, into the pointless. Supplicated angels' wings are growing onto the cars. The sky is too wide for this crowd and anxiously pinches its bottom. And breaks wind. What? Please! Let it defend itself! Against fear. Against the rush of the flying Alzette valleys. Which is brought about by the growing wings. Growth's stop and go! Home-comer's carillon. They fight it with jangling teeth and nails. The escaping. Icy chilliness sprouts from the farting sky hole. The arising mist of the valleys obstructs this sight to my sensitive eyes. I recognize panic! But these jammed fears are too much. Too many feathers grow at the same time. This time knows nothing more. No rules! No mercy! The borders of the tasteless cross hard shoulders left behind on the Adolphe Bridge. Of time left behind. Which stands still! Surrendering? For good? No. Just! What is that? It is itself that runs away. Cowardly flop! Passive bouncer! Professional liar! Bought disperser! Ridiculous disposer! Time passing by is mediocre. Good times are pinched. Wings are trimmed. The secretly growing ones! My robot arms cannot endure this spectacle any longer. I cannot just watch how the cars become hypocritical. I get incredibly busy. Must clip the wings of every single one of these swinging, home-coming cars. A brutal endeavour considering the number. That approaches me. In the jam. I bother with details. The feather scraps fly, torn out, through the arising fog into the valley. These wide angels are stoned. The Hudson River pokes nervously with bridge pillars and skyscraper reflections into its riverbed. He knows of what the stoned angels who fall off from above are capable. What I am speaking about? The American water bleeds from all this poking. And I struggle courageously and unconditionally through the fowl meat of the Adolphe Bridge. Werewolves dance chaotically through my efforts. Now it's me who will not allow them to escape. The patient. The hiding ones. They should cast my unredeemable lot. If I do not get to New York the regular way, they should go to seed in the jam wolf of my disappointment. Armless, the indignated Terminator clinches to my tearing-out fury. "What are you doing there? Stop it! Leave it! It makes no sense! You won't change anything! You won't do it! You are a loser. You slump the whole evening. The whole world. You do not understand the story. You are out of place!" Only this underestimation carries me to crowd-blemishing top performances. What should I have misunderstood? This place? This text? This jam! This Adolphe Bridge! All the bridges in the world are Adolphe Bridges! This is your final destination! Hurry up! This is the road to Guantanamo! This place where is no justice? These disastrous consequences? A hole bores into my soul. The text shoots out of the mincer of desperation. Ant-legged sentences are convulsed with laughing in the dumdum bullets of the dead dreamed longings. Resolving, as soon as one approaches them! At the moment it is inaccessible. The fog of the growing angel's wings squeezes every way out. Do I tear out of them, these cowardly jam standers, these confounded wings, so that they do not escape? Of them who undertake absolutely nothing to help me in the progress of my purpose? Or do I let them grow up and allow them to fly away? To the head slaughterers? The skysick persons? To the paradise of the Terminators? Nevertheless, this is ridiculous! Belief in escape? Nobody will ever find it out. The fact that I have got stuck. In getting stuck! I only need to push the button and it would be over. It would be gone. The jam. The lot. The bridges. The targeting. Push the button! Man! Now go ahead! I am the murderer of my story. The chapter killer! I do not do it for myself. Too long have I condoned its making the rules. Its defining time. My story! It must be over. I must shred it. The skysick angel's wings which are growing on every home-comer. Suddenly! It is me who must dissolve it. Now! The jam. All of it! It is me who has absolutely no sense. Of patience. Of such humor. I can do what I want. Blah-blah-blah! So I am no Alzette, no Hudson River. Stand with legs apart above the Alzette Valley. Like haughty twin towers. I am a peed jet of water. Which sweats out of longing fireman eyes. Cuts gigantic firebreaks. Through all obstacles. Through which rivers of indignation are going to lurch about like insignificant stroller' steps. Afterwards complete loneliness! On trampled paths. Losing oneself! In high spirits. No sooner said than done! Yet the first gray crowds of crazed horse powers gallop through the forbidden shades of time standing still. Dusty clouds rush at my face. Angels' feathers stick to my sweated effort. I must be damn harmless-looking! Like a plush toy in a plush zoo. The mutating home-comers believe, I am one of them. I do not get it! My genetic code behaves strangely. Like a sausage. One with an infinite number of knots. A knausage. Is stretched in my insanity like a Lincoln-Stretch-Sedan. The driver holds the door open. Terminator gets in. "Good evening, sir!" All just a game? A little drollery? "Drive off! Follow this thought!" I can barely expect it. The hunt begins. Unthinking home-comers protest against the slaughter of defenceless chimeras. Pointless! Terminator bangs pitilessly. It splashes everywhere. The angels' feathers blush. And run like used tampons through the excited mess of the jam. The Adolphe Bridge becomes the Red Bridge. The Suicide's Bridge. The tampons jump desperately into the depth. I have the feeling that it changes nothing. Nothingness changes nothing! Whether they jump or not, the mass of the home-comers remains always the same. Patience in the reception camp. Buffer zone between space and time. No-man's-land of the mass dreams. They obey weird laws. The bridges are the rule. The home-comers the tampons. Time the superfluous blood. And I the bad mood. Mimosa! The unfertilized story. Whom does it concern? Should it go on? Is there an adequate answer to all of it? The blood of the mass flows down the brook. And, nevertheless, it is as if the lumps of the bridge ventilated themselves. On my clotty skin there rules indescribable chaos. Feathery uptightness hardens my palpitation. It drums against the walls of the sausage. It bends the spaces of time. That is left to me. The jammed thoughts untidily stream. Pile up one onto the other. Smack the salami one by one. And creep away in dead-ending blind lanes. As a precaution. As if the knots of my scrotum hair were being undone at the other end. The knots of my sausage. Me too a sausage? A slice? Softened, monstrous illusion. Let them have me! Home-coming floaters, blood corpses, angels of death prepare for mass execution. Going once. Going ultimately? I do not want to admit it. The news disabuses me. The events are being broadcast. Live. Unplugged! It is unstoppable. It lurches through the events. I am fucked. Hurray! The lot has been drawn. Hurray! The trip starts. Hurray! New York, I am coming. Hurray! The band begins to play. The fun is over. Past is past. The Alzette spreads its legs and its moisture devours my luscious sentences. On its naked skin I begin to swirl. In my back a crazed bridge attacks. "There he bolts!" Amok makes itself at home. Home-comers mushroom up from nowhere. Women from behind become mad furies. Terminators God's warriors. Horse powers cannibals. Ant legs become meaningless letters. Half-open window panes become straight-jackets. Rear-view mirrors become betrayers. Bumpers become child abusers. Radio waves become tsunamis. Traffic jam predictions become horror stories. Weather forecasts become the ten Commandments. Closing times become life-ending knots.

Front seat passengers become head slaughterers. And you become the accessory! The toady. Cheater. Pursuer. I knew it! All of it becomes too much! All of it attacks my neck with a combined leaping sentence. The wrinkles of the story pounce on me. Slap me between the legs of the stupid Alzette. However, I am of elected defiance. Clap back. Flying on the back. Into the robot hands! Bravo!! Of enthusiasm. Bravo!! I come! I escape! Is that all? That's what it was? A bridge collapsing onto me stuffed with jam idiots should lure me out of my reserve. Hello? Already forgotten? I am the chosen one! I clinch to the fight-experienced suicide thoughts which bounce around like alert snowflakes in the roundabout of the general stupidity. Stand still! I am the applause of the hitting tears of an armless Terminator. The home-comers are horrified. I am a star! I have to leave here. I must go to New York. I must go onto the Brooklyn Bridge. I feel it. It only attracts me there. Namely right now! Powered by this storm. And here I splash in the slime of this new sausage. Devour its glowing heat. That of its cooking fury. At me! At my outbreaks! Am sucked into a home-comer's marsh. Like in the scream of a painting by Munch. Irrevocably! Famous! Finally! That's what you think! Have you forgotten my robot arms? Which I can claw into mountains of patient meat. Which spread out in front of me like a longing past. A mouldy slice. Sausage? The story? The bubbling Alzette Valley? So to speak, lost time. Fluent sadness. A burst bowel has more fun with life. An overdose of cockiness overpowers my sickness.

”Oh how nice is the Alzette!“ Mountains of meat sing hack. Above me! Show me their backs. Fly. Over me! All of it slews. The scream of the ladies is enticing. Sucks the mouth of the Hudson River. On the Brooklyn Bridge there stand the leggiest ladies of New York and scream hysterically. ”He comes!“ The bridge shakes. A ladies jam! They pull off their clothes and throw them in the river. Only to rescue me. I only see naked American ladies. Long arms and legs. Shaven onto the edge. Of the vulva. It drags me there, without fail. It already splashes in my balls. These are for a change fetching troublemakers. A proper diversion. Hopefully! And if not, I don’t give a damn. Should they stink! It is all right with me. Better than croaking on the Alzette Bridge. Climb promptly and purposefully up my steel looks. Time rods! Fossilized longing strings. Spread my fat kisses with waving dick and calm nonchalance out into the staddle-legged arrival night. Brooklyn shines brightly. The river shines. Time resembles a last sparkle of luck. In the stiff irises of death. Free of wrinkles! Slick like an eel! Summed up! Greasy! Humid! Pushing! 6 pm. The last tear jumps overboard. Original time jump of a spinner. The Atlantic slops over. Time curls. Fun-loving! Jumps amused into the fresh meat. As if it was me! The laughter. The wave. The novella. Of the arrived Alzette. Down to the ground of the earth. Where I get out. Following the nonsense of a jam episode. Featherweightly I fly over the bridges and oceans of the appointments. Dazedly I subdue the flying seconds to a precise schedule.

And I do not recognize the danger. The knot spots! The upshots of the bridges! There, where they hide. The envious people. The fervent jealous. The regular. The patient ones. Which like vice squads in the firmly lashed knots are standing at the upshots of the Brooklyn Bridge. While I believe to rage into the long legs of the American ladies. The knots harden. That is the only certainty! Contracting. Like a shrinking dick. A burnt sausage. The ladies pant. Under the pressure of the new traffic rules. 6 pm: Rule number 9: More and more rules! It gets complicated. I don't care! I need it. The panting of the ladies. Of the rules. What should I care whose origin it is. If it is about naked survival. About mine. That of time? In a foreign world? Of the rules? In a stolen time? A stung sharp second? In which all of it turns? Too fast? In which it is about all or none of it? All of it is okay to me. Too much has happened. The story is bursting at the seams. Time drops its anchor. Superfluous ballast is abandoned. The purpose is reached! The lot is redeemed. I am the happy winner of a trip into the convulsions. Of the future. Now here I am. Faster than the sound. Of fear. Devastation. Out for me? Only chaos. Alzette Valley people! Before me lies New York. At my feet. Brightly illuminated. Naked and screaming. Encircled. Wet and greedy. Shaved from top to toe. The long legs. Of the drawn out ladies. Nothing is random. The Brooklyn Bridge is closed. The ladies are cooped-up. Full of expectation. Freedom waves clemently over here. As usual. All of it runs like clockwork. All of it is ready. The vice squad is on the ball. SNAP! I love it! SNAP! The home-comers are bogged down into the hungry seas. SNAP! Time rears up in vain. An accumulation of riderless horse powers. SNAP! The ants bridge over the time tankers. SNAP! Terminator buries himself under the broken stones of the perfidious Adolphe Bridge. Turns a well-functioning blind eye to the Statue of Liberty. SNAP! The car wrecks are smug about a lumpy knot. SNAP! A memorial of common sense! Of progress! In the middle of the Alzette Valley. A dust knot. The serrating of the knots really makes no sense. But I love it! My sentences serrate into the story and point at me cheekily. They can afford this! Already join the end of the queue. Where the serrating gets knotted. SNAP! The story is a black hole. In a black slice. SNAP! The zero rivets on my neck. Curious? Arriving is out! SNAP! Ground Zero is in! SNAP! The old rules are out! Get drunk with the nectar of my dreams. Profoundly disappointed about my slipping through. My escape! The weather forecasts hang in the air. The loops in the traces of time. The matter with the jam has been sorted out. SNAP! The few pieces of debris squeeze out of my scars. But there is something far worse! Than sick and tired American ladies' legs. Up to the navel shaved ones! Which embrace you. Like eels an empty horse skull. My devotion to them is smashing. Disturbing stuff shimmers in the far distance. In the tip of an unreal horizon gleam knots. Menacing views! Annoying hair is exterminated without hesitation. Plucked. Outlawed. Voluntarily.

Really. All of it is real! Odoriferous fresh meat. No rotten meat. No sausage meat. Thus it appears! Thus deceptive is the image. Perfumed desire overcomes me. Kept ecstasy discharges. My pathetic robot arms shake silently. Lose themselves in the rainforests of the embraced hair splendour. The juice of the melting lipsticks embalms my shaken skin leftovers. It all happens by itself. Nothing holds me back! All of it overwhelms. Gets drunk. Piles up. To a heap of uncontrolled sentences. Into the Hudson River. Although! Still I hear the constant bubbling of the sinking troublemakers. Into the sinking Alzette. Into this sinking evening light. Indestructible, these home-comers! In the immense seas behind me it bubbles without end. In those the Alzette gets lost definitively and ridiculously. Dissolves! Empties. Without respite! Like a slaughtered sow. A future GUESS-WHAT? The sausage. The end. The world. A drop of time in the bucket of elapsing. A second's dust particle in the eye of a head slaughterer. Who simply looks away. Disgusted! And runs into his own knife. Point of honor! How dare he? How can all of it shift so fast? On the slice of the events. Do I think! And let myself go on Brooklyn Bridge. Like a struggling prisoner. Let myself float. Fall. Undress. Prod to and fro. Hug. I fly from the embrace of one leggy beauty to the next. On my back. Masterly. The sky always reliable in the blind spot of view. A bad starting point. A cheap emergency rest area. As a precaution! I never know what could come. An ounce of prevention is the mother of all stand-still. On the bridges. Of the stamping home-comers. Which catapult their sluggishness to Brooklyn. In these smooth women's legs. For deception's sake. They try to deceive me. Lead me to believe something. So that I imagine being in New York! They pull my ears. So that I believe in myself! Play with my toes. Knead my thoughts. My scars get caught in their braids. Whisper mysterious messages to me. "Don't be foolish! Don't let yourself be fooled! Not all of it is as it seems! You should reverse! Don't let yourself be seduced! We are innocent of what happens. We do not belong to your clumsy story. But! We cannot help it. We have no choice. We are observed. Look, at the end of the bridge they stand! They are no traffic knots! They are THEM! They are out to get you. They are just waiting to turn you in! Take care, DARLING!" Sure! No problem! Kiss Kiss. Is a piece of cake. A motherfucking hot dog. Flipping the sausage, before it burns! I feel how the pressure becomes bigger. The heat rises. Sky high! Feel that the story gives me no chance. Slips! On the ice of heartlessness. All of it is too much! All of it is over! The legs of the slippery ladies press closer together. The dripping lipsticks run me dry. Ice-cold looks tap into my heart. Then the unforeseen occurs! They suddenly rush to the other side of the bridge. Tear the icicles of their looks out of the muffled beats of my heart. Pull one wet devil after the other from the gray every-day life of the water. One jam survivor? After the other? What is this suppose to mean now? So I am not the only one! All of it only imposture? Illusion? All for nothing? A slice? A sausage? A knot? The home-comers share my fate? The entire jam has survived? Hit the jackpot? I am not the chosen one? The sausage not a real one? I am a nothing? A zero? Nowhere come across? Am stuck? Nothing has changed? Adolphe Bridge equal to Brooklyn Bridge? The ladies only hacked meat! HACK? HACK? They who now pull Terminator by his arm stumps from the dripping floods? Excuse me! What's this bullshit? Scum! Plagiarism! Irony of fate? Same scenario! Same story! Last chapter! Showdown! Nonsense till the bitter end. No more fun! Deliberately! I work my balls off and Terminator rakes in? On the Adolphe Bridge? In New York? The jam is hard on my heels? The home-comers hang like jump-jacking haemorrhoids from my arse? Oh no, not that! Should I bleed to death backwards? And I should be content with the residues of the world? Prove lousy patience? Share my drawn lot? Hide my purposes? Change the navigation system? Accept the rules? Not so! Not cornering me! Not irritating me! I not rectum! Not constipation! Not jam! I back air-man! Dreamer! Poet! Word catcher! Not laxative! Not saviour! I chosen! Exception! Taking time out! Sucking freedom! Like mother's milk. Then smooching! The left-over ladies up to the end of the leggy bridge. The unshaven ones, too. With the shorter legs. The patience of the home-comers, too. It does not work out otherwise. Which stick to me. Like the jam plague! Fine dust! Death-driven déjà vus! If need be! I must continue. Have no choice! Lengthen them. The long legs. The viscous chewing gum home-comers. The distorted seconds. Enjoy them! As long as they have taste. The experiences. The inevitable. The endless. Random ones. In the end, all of it has its order. To have! All of it to end once. The sausage locked up in the corner. Whether here in New York or there in the Alzette Valley. In the end, one of the knots must burst. Time must suffocate in my voluptuous fury. And woe is you, your looks walk in one of my areas. In one of my sentences. When the dam breaks. The bowels have had enough. And all of it shoots. Sentences! From a rusted gun. The way of the world. Rectally hidden. Recollections of patient nothingless. Pending past. Blood-satisfied home-comers. Time standed still! Ready for battle! Coordinated future. Piece-worked. In the headcheese. In slinky traced loops. Mushy thoughts! In ownerless brains. Armless figures! In wrong films. Stood hours! In endless jams. Got over seconds! In toxic lipsticks. Full-punched slices! With any information. Warnings. Predictions. False alarms. Searches. Much too leggy ladies! In hairless underwear. Meanwhile patient idiots are trampling on my soul. Swarms of ants dreams creep away into the hollow sentences. It trembles on my naked skin. So that it is shaking under me. Like a broken beaten heart. In the murderous hands of a knotted gang of skysick home-comers. Gathering together at the other end of Brooklyn Bridge. To stop me. Me! To brake. Me! To a standstill. To force. To cease. Me? The high flyer! The Springer! Absorbing the spritzer of the last drop of the blood which it loses! This beaten heart. As if it was imperative to survive. In this naked ladies' sausage. This new ladies' jam. This werewolfly Adolphe Bridge. Now Adolphe, now Brooklyn. In this unsatisfied time. These crooked rules. These constant desires. Of renewable escaping. Flying fleeing! From the common fancilessness. Out of an atypical tire pressured world in excess. With softening crumple zone. Without exceptional poetry. Which stands a little bit more. Than dilapidated laws. And dull slogans. That are as empty as the dried farts of a common home-comer off the peg of the prison of a crumbling stone bridge. Which nobody wants to have. Or just because of it! In any case, one thing is clear: The bridges which I bridge are not of stone! Have no ends. And no purposes! Are no mini-sausages. I bridge them only in the spaces of stand-still seconds. Back beating ones! Into the walking attempts of paralysing letters. Into the steps of unmasterly outbreaks. Into the leg losing of bridging ants. Into the bucking of arrogant horse powers. Into the sluggishness of your reading eyes. The fluttering of your compassionate looks. The fat of your brain. If you have made it up to here. In this babbling! Tied up by this screaming flood of sense. On the bridge above a miserable valley. Not even that bad! I award a special prize to your patience. This is a super performance! You are nuts! Respect! Suggest, nevertheless, simply forgetting about these bridges! It's no use! They are too hollow. Too anchored. In the story. Forget Adolphe Bridge! Forget Brooklyn Bridge! Forget the literal bridges! Remain where you are! Stand still! FREEZE! Nobody budges! Halt! Or I shoot! Aimlessly around. At random! Like a maniac. Anyhow! Who runs out of spittle. In this long-term jam. Of the manned eternities. Where the bridge of my exorcized dreams does not even upset a shadow? I bridge one stand-still second after the other. Throw me into it. Into the stuff! Into this empty bowel. Like the exsanguinated pig into the eager length of the sausage. Lie down on the scarred back and let it slip. Skip! Fly! Over, through, into me! The event of the stand-still! The stillness of the story. Which secludedly meditates under the jam of realisation. So-called hermit! Haughty shaman! Foodless. Waterless. Alzetteless! Nothing I would prefer more. Than this sight. For whatever reason. It is incomprehensible enough. However, it is not enough to calm me down. To interpret time at the exact point. Time, which casts a scarred shadow. Onto the Alzette. Meaningless! The Hudson River is not luckier. And the shadeless Terminator has even, armless and meaningless, reached the promised land. And cheers them on. The smart-alecks. Which suddenly are after me as if all of it were up to me. In my dripping hands. They! The chasers of the missed opportunities. Of the hours missed in jams. Of the innocent burglars in their tolerated queue world. They! The smart-wankers embroiled in knotspots! Only waiting for me to get entangled. Trespass! Tuck! Make a mistake. One too many! Do not observe the rules. Stride clangorously loud over the bridge. STRIDE! CLANGOROUSLY LOUD! ARE YOU RECEIVING? Combine impossibilities. Bridge them! Book them! Words which don't want to have anything to do with each other. Everlasting enemies! Sentences which hate each other. Vendetta! Palpitation! Thoughts which fight against each other. Inside the molten time mush. Gladiators! Survival chanceless! Tripping steps which become entangled. Anting letters which throw themselves in the Alzette Valley. Like into a pale shroud. Plucked out! Lubberly! Woozily! To land as an android in the river of time which trickles out from the leaking bladder of a much too patient trouble-maker's knot. Playful showing-off! Mine! Unskillful sausage bursting! Mine? Attention! Stay behind me, OK? Is safer. Who knows what else is going to happen. Inside this story. Which cannot end. Because it is never going to be one. None of it is true! Of this heap of life. This endless sausage. Which cannot even come up with illusions. A miserable endeavour. This attempt! To get across. To arrive somewhere. At least once! In the torn-apart arms of the agape jam grimaces? At the end of the bridge? In Brooklyn? Where I want to go. Wherever! To start a new life? Must this be? Must I absolutely get across! Climb over them? Those, who like the vice squadmen start to tug me. To torment me. To dismantle me. To tear me to pieces. Each sentence is examined! Each jump of the springer scrutinized. After all, there are certain rules which have to be followed scrupulously. Certain laws! Paralysing poison! "Be reasonable! Don't be silly! Don't talk rubbish! All of this makes no sense ! Is useless gossip! We will not tolerate it. It dirties our patience. It disturbs us! It is out of the question! Must be destroyed! Degenerates our life expectancies. Break his fingers! Nail him to the bridge pillar! Burn his haste! Knot him! Jail him!“ They are ready! They are firmly decided. Their patience appears to be stumped. The culprit is found. The jam criminal surrounded. The enemy detected. The purposes are set. Time is overstretched. 6 pm: How much longer? Dead dreamed! Now it is about the actual sausage. Withstanding? Game is over! I am fucked. If a miracle doesn't happen. In these skysick times. Of the superfluous troublemakers. À gogo! Who dissolve in mile-long queues to make their hateful circles. Like loops of reason. Like beds of the Alzettes. Like valleys of moaning. Like tricks in the book. Like bottlenecks of the connections. They knot themselves together. Insolubly! Tighter and tighter. More and more pitilessly. More and more firmly. There is no escape. No river! The party can begin! The knots are anchored. Pulled around my neck snapping at air. Gallows! Home-comers! Bridges! Long-running jam! Jail! Rules! Schedules! Appointments! Purposes! All of it chokes on my terror about the desolation of this inapt world. Which makes me sweat. Which does not loosen the distortion of the finger knots. One can only imagine resolution. If this is going to be the last straw. If! Once again! And over and over again! Without respite! Without considering! On call! With full power. Regardless of the consequences. Namely now! Anything still goes! A later does not exist. Later the story is blind. Later barely makes sense. Earlier this was still nonsense! But now it is a sausage. Earlier? A firm knot which takes our freedom away. A period! Later? A strange knot. Of time! Which finishes us off. And you think, you are the law in the flesh? Want to hunt me down? Finish the story? Stop time? Destroy the Adolphe Bridge? Renounce me? Bundle up the incoherent? Dock Terminator's arms again? Restore the home-comers into the jam? Punish the past seconds? See Chimeras running away? Sure! Go ahead! Spin that shit! The ladies' long legs already spin. Over enthusiasm! While watching. This farce! How I am doing. In this jam! From where there seems to be no way out in spite of all attempts. Unless failing. Absolute failing. Absolute art! All the same where! Got stuck. All the same how! That is not the question. That is fact! A hackfact. Snapfact! Fuck! An endless state. Full of gravity. Grave of consequences. Barely to endure. Cruel! And damn tight! The air is scarce. Time presses. Greedily. Small-minded. Unanimously. The jam does not admit it. That it goes on. The slackness! Of the promise. Of the confused choice of words. As if there was a choice. There isn't! Believe me! What will be, will have to be. It bangs as it must bang! Down onto the story. The impact of a suicidal springer! From one of the tinkered bridges of the deedless in rank and file standing around troublemakers into the restricting valley of the remaining time span. Trailing all of it behind! Dismantling all of it! Calling all of it into naked questions! The jump into emptiness the only possible miracle. To escape from the mob! From the mutation of the home-comers! Which simulate barking vice dogs like the blowflies do. ”RAF! RAF! RAF! We will get you!“ They swear absolute obedience to revenge! Revenge to the impatient. To the enemy of the state. To the troublemaker of the troublemakers! Revenge to the failure! What is this noise? This nonsense? Nobody dies here, before I say it! Not without me! Bridge death! Jam death! Slice death! Sausage death? Do I look death-driven? One doing it in the sausage? Do I firmly keep the stuff of moderating in hand? That of the happening? Onto this bridging around? Hello! And how should I succeed? Can only I disentangle it? I, the chosen one! With the steely arms of a robot-like saviour on the trunk of a harmless stroller. I! The stepper. The scandalizer. The one doomed to it! To make the clot more. I must anticipate the advancement. Define it. You must trust me! Times are hard. A fossilized sausage of the past. Order must be. Spoke the sausage! Someone has to do it. Spoke the knot! One is the dummy-dummy. The shot one. And already they are ready. The vice squads. Laugh my downfall up their sleeves. Spread bridgely. The bridge endings pat, so that they crumble. In the models of the bridge stones running out. So that it can lead to nothing. What they plan! Since their art of poetry is miserable. Stale. Worn out. Stuck. A thick dust particle. Adapted to the drawn levelless lot of the jam announcements. In all the stale time? No miracle! Onto which I could clinch. In the hope of stopping it. The Catch-22 situation! Which rolls towards me with honking protest. An avalanche of secret jam epicures which tries to undermine me. Me, the unique back airman. The roughly scarred one. Just when I stopped it. Believing in miracles! Rendering homage to the skysicknesses of the patient in-line standers. These bouncing directors! In front of impervious misfortune! It is too compact! Comes up to me like a frozen state. Is a hardly playable slice. According to which the hostile mood spreads out onto the fragile bridge. The mash of the sausage glides from the reins. It becomes slimy. Queasy. Awful. Slip danger! Into the arms of desire. To chop me! Now that I am busy being grated into this mash. It starts to end! That of the sausage. The end. The world. The knot of the drawn lot. And this on a day like today. An incredibly nice day! One could suppose. I supposed! Perfect for a walk home of a late afternoon. Through the patient fine dust of a stone bridge. Which is closer to decay than the afternoon. Over there to the desired travel agency. Or to a reading. With a begun story between the stuttering teeth. The naughty ones. Sealed ones. They try to keep the wild sentences of fright under control. Fright which is once more sweating. Because of the piled up failure. In burning out! A herd of alarmed horse powers. Which float disoriented to and fro. On the run! Before themselves! In their whirled up dust! Which rebels into a menacing and impenetrable cloud of frazzle. And wraps me in frightening vacuum! In the transition of the rush-hour traffic. In the daily jam. In the perfidious embrace of the home-coming! The biggest luxury of the burghers. The Adolphes of the

Adolphe Bridge! Which bites its pillars like false teeth into the valley of tears of the Alzette. A bleeding mask into the yawn of the dead lion. It has to drag one somewhere! This tohubohu of the tired hours which shudder in my versified life. No place for staying! A dusty playground! The story of this sausage! The sparrows whistle it already from the roofs of the sloshed column of cars. From the conceited skulls of the red lions. The wheeled canned insanity meat of the furious home-comers. In the primate homes of the customs! There is no miracle exactly at 6 pm! If there has never been! But no panic! That was it! The last of the broken rules assumes shape. Great! Since that is no more going to become a decent story. It is only a tiresome developing work. An impossible getting there! The desire to put an end to that. A solving! Daily! Of the navel knots. On the ending border of time. Hardly conceivable! The attempt to escape! To increase it! An extinguishing of the pilot flame. Of the fire which burns me down daily. On special days. Today! Now! Here! On the point exactly! On this slice! Ant leggly precise! In the midst of time. Of the home-comers! The skeletons! The enemies of the late seconds. Of the scanty flames. In the Alzette Valley. In which gobs of lurching home-comers start to burn. Patiently inflamed. Like goodbye castles! Evaporating tears! Dusty glow clouds. Overheated stand-still engines. Exhaust-inhaling junkies in the stand-still death agony. They run after me! As if I had the stuff which accelerates their dreams. As if I was the worm-hole with the tunnel vision into another time. Towards another place. I? The sausage hole! The twisted bridge space. The bent second of their home-coming. However, unfortunately, there is a problem! I am the chosen one. Extremely unsteady! If I am stuck. Into the exotic matter of a home-comer's mass. Have other worries! Then to let myself get caught by sausage eaters. Am not playing the set example! Am not ending as a warning! However, they insist on the fact that one has to respect them. In their skysick jam. Which they seem to enjoy. Because it is such truth as the gospel. Theirs, to be sure! However, I am not really so sure about that. Whether they get to catch me in my fast-as-lightning mental leaps. My impatience is as slippery as their slimy front seat passenger's grin. "So get in! Drive you across to the other side of the bridge. You can rely on me. I'll help you out of there. The jam looks worse than it is. Believe me! I know it like my trouser pocket." I want to believe this, you wanker. But now they have barricaded the bridge ends. With their creeping around. And under these circumstances there is no getting through. Not like this! And I have also already checked off the thing with the miracles. Remains to me only trick 17: Sublimation! I must sublimate myself out of there. Make myself unfathomable! Invisible! Incomprehensible! Illegible! As if this was so easy! To UN be! Not to exist. To act as if I was another. Hell! For example! Amaze. (Not hell! Do not exaggerate it! I am not at all so bad.) Because jam eaters cannot do both at the same time: Being astonished and acting! I must mislead them in the boundless madness of the Adolphe Bridge's downfall which puffs out on the horizon around this eventide like popping poppy, which is sick of the radiance from yesterday and tired of the junk of a disastrous drug that hangs out of its stalk. I must seed the accumulated jam dots into the scratches and joints of the stones and skeletons, in the worthless hope that they become anthropophagous and caoutchouc melting plants of revenge. Exterminating giants of a completely demented entertainment show. Must split the core of the standing time. So that it can freely develop again. Can explode. Make its straightjacket crack. Can take revenge. Time revenge is worse than vendetta. The time bomb is ticking! The jam duty suffocating! It is bowing to this pressure. And even in the seconds is too much fury. And already armless Terminators and leggy women shout from the shaven distance of unbridgeable New York: ”NOTHING IS IMPOSSIBLE!“ I say only one thing: So one gets depressed and sad if they shout like the skysick people and drown out the tick of the time bomb. ”Hey!“ I scream back, ”What is this for? Have you swigged this in one of the time holes of the advertising breaks? What about a little bit of imagination? None of it is impossible! Really? I am profoundly disappointed. Honestly! The only impossible thing here is you. And you are all of it! Troublemakers! None of it is impossible? I cannot believe it ...!“ I must really do something. Have no choice. Chosen is chosen! Temporizing does not work. It is ticking! One must find the way out. And from me you expect it? ME?

The most unclear unthinker? In spite of second-long glancing nothing burns more under my nails than incoherent tirades, a constant roaring which only waits to get hammered. By sausaged reading brain. Yours! Burned out moments! Ours! Horse-strengthened invasion troops! Yours! Inevitable defeats! However, what do I care? Actually? Except that I am stuck in the middle of it? Like the bite in the sausage! And try to interpret from far away the wobbling of the bridgehead. Want to understand it anyhow. A bow? No! These are the movements of small maggots. They slobber over themselves. Bubble out of excitement. On the corner of a decayed sausage. It is the ticking of the second pointer of a patient time bomb. Furious faltering of an overacidified jam. Whose acid overflows. Menacing. Corrosive! Wheeled misfortune. Black! 4-legged sitting out. Infinite sweating out. Leggy bumming around. Uncertain waiting around. Stressed silence. Rushed rest. Before the rush. Of the home-comers. Brilliant disaster mood. The spearheads approach! The fatal shot already trickles from their syringe. The leggy ladies laugh a tear of luck between the bumcrack. Terminator bares his stump teeth. Bit by bit it becomes tight. In the traffic jam paradise! Always it is too tight! All over! To me, in any case! Time runs crappily down my temples. 6 pm: The countdown has begun. For eternities. And not only it! It bangs. All over! In the universe. In the occupied territories of the cars. The barricaded bridge ends of the skysick dream factories. The sausage knots of the patient. The travel agencies of the released ones. On the bending and breaking of the leggy Brooklyn Bridge strollers. Even below in the blazing Alzette Valley the flames pound enraged against its upright abysses. Like the haughty laughter of confirmed spectators. Clap! Clap! The unexcelled home-comers's scum are clapping! They throw themselves deeply into it. Into the ravage of the minutes. The violating of time's circumference. The drowning of the opportunities. To change it! The chased hiding. The constant observing. To remove! To transform it! Into a sublimated trip. Into a boundless time. In which the future is not only a substitution of the past. Have a look at my substitution! A constrained moment which sprinkles, deeply, inhaled the lungs of the honking scenery. The fool's theater of the Adolphe Bridge! The unused jester's license of its occupants! The first signs of the jam inferno are there! Spanned like a spider's net! And I am the caught fly which flounders and immediately buzzes, let it be rescued from here as soon as possible, especially since it is a star! This is inacceptable! It has to have some say. The fly! Before the spider poisons and consumes me! However, this process can last. It is not yet done. I recognize the precise point in time when it must happen. Precisely! A few steps from here! Barely a Terminator's arm away. And I have no more time to lose. In this story of failing. The obsession of the word crooks. To which an immediate end should also be put. To this imposition which I imagine having to inform you about at all costs. I also have nothing better to do. At this moment! In this sausage! At which end I see you observing me. Thus! You want to know it? Are so to speak virtually keen on finding out whether here and now anything at all happens? Understand! In the end, you have ideas! Appointments! Expectations! In me! In the end! Of the story! The sausage! And in what else, please? Nevertheless, I already told you that you can challenge my word. LITERALLY! Take it like I give it to you. It is only a walk in the late afternoon. This day ran out a long time ago. The sentences of the story are exhausted. Spare sentences! Ail because of the packages of the blanched pages. The trouble-makers are already almost at home. Almost! And still you trample with startled look through the delusive footnotes of my jam episode as if you were doing me a favour. As if you could foresee its end. Still search for a sense. In this jam! Try to untie the knots. Good luck! You try to give me, so to speak, page for page a chance to please you. To take part! In you! The jam! The sausage! Oh believe me, I try damn hard. But I am nobody who is able to match the uncontrolled time struggles. As if I was in the stream of an Alzette blown out to an ocean I flounder into my collapse and see the world the wrong way round. Drowned! And from below I see the cracked trunk of the Adolphe Bridge and crowds of into this trunk stung women's legs which dive in vain for me. With sharpened toenails. Like the spits of a meat fondue they stab at me. It is a heavenly sight. I see only the long legs as if they hung like kissing lips out of the sick and tired neck of the sky. The rest of the ladies does not seem to be anymore. This must be the beginning of the madness into which this jam drives me bit by bit. If it goes on this way, I'll tell you! How it was! Then I make a story out of that. Then I'll explain all of it. Every detail! Then I'll do research on every weather forecast and jam announcement. Analyze the jam behaviour of every home-comer. How the story developed. How it happened. This daily traffic jam. The crumbling of the bridge. Then maybe I'll also tell you the story about the encounter with the lady from the cart behind and how our family failed. And why I met, stuck in a window gap, a Terminator. I hope you know who Terminator is? Otherwise you can stop reading on immediately! IS THIS CLEAR? In any case, leggy ladies are always worth a story. No matter whether clearly or unclearly! It has to do with the ants. With sublimation! To express it once clearly: Ant legs are written letters. Quasi poems! And the long shaven ladies' legs are the cradle of inspiration of a poet of my kind. Thus a poem comes into being. These legs are the bridges to the world. Sleek and shaven. Fragrant. Then it rustles and prickles. The letters slowly grow up into words. These are the tiny hairs. After a few days they are harvested. Ready! And thus they hang in my perception. In my sky. And threaten me and my jammed dreams. Are fed up of letting themselves get harvested by me. To be my bridges which I build to reach from myself to you. For example! That's why they came together. Threw me into the Alzette. Into the braid knots of age. Of the Adolphe Bridge. And in an unfeasible story. And they have turned away from me. To save Terminator from the floods of the Hudson River. Now that they know how it works. And I stand bared and flabbergasted on this stupid bridge in this persistent jam and progress neither forward nor backward. Time has stopped definitively and the seconds wait only to freeze me out of their beloved jam. Because I don't respect them enough. Because I start to rampage. Must get out! Must get free. Cannot take it anymore! This madness, this nonsense, this affected behaviour, this bragging. This bend. There nothing is liquid. There nothing is loose. This is not going to work out. There is no progress. These are only standing points. Which won't let me go anymore. Surround! Time-fattened dust particles of a bridge belonging to the wrong time! I schlep the isolated seconds like blood reserves with myself. Am a tick fallen into a time hole, which greedily sips it empty. The soaked up bridge along with the passengers. In my delusion all of it is possible. A cruel onus. An emptiness. A fascinating choice of evacuated time spots which spreads out in front of me. Stranded sand at the sea of hope. Between Alzette and Hudson River. And which are all alike. All sit in the same boat. In the same mincer. With the hungry time blackheads. The pimples in the hoggish bridge face. Which spreads out in the grimaces of the troublemakers. A true flood of senses. "Gorge the sausage!" They scream again. "GORGE IT!" And now you too are starting! To shake off your fat. "It is only mash! Is not so bad. Why are you getting so excited? So that I feel sick.

From your torrent of words. Do it like I do! Accept it! Have patience! Don't be a spoilsport! Shut the fuck up! Stop, finally, hammering your impossible story into the keyboard! Have some compassion with us! You behave like a chosen one! You are getting on my nerves! You are not better than us. Thus stand your ground! Line up! Your place in rank and file has already been reserved for years. Place Number 7: The jam loves you! You belong to us. Are one of us!" That's what you think! But only you! I in contrast page up and down your abided restart through the evening jam like through a cheap telenovella. Through the sausaged container of your expired clingfilms. Through a football arena of anthropophagous Taliban fighters. Through your automobile love and your on-schedule betrayal. It leaves me colder and colder. The whole thing! All of it! The TOO MUCH! So much that the leaving-me-cold becomes an addiction! I am so addicted meanwhile, almost obsessed, that I sprint down your dreadfully depilated back with frozen indifference. To arrive even faster! At the nodal point of the inaccessible purposes. At the end! Of your sluggishness! In the arse! Of the world! At the end of the bridge railing. Of the Adolphe Bridge. Which spreads out into infinity. Like the pulled filament of spittle between the excited lips of two separating kisses. Knotting ones, which never want to stop dissolving. Kissed spittle which simply cannot do any more! Than to spread out thin Golden Gate threads. Which are simply no more good in it! In finding common grounds. In loving each other.

Joining! Conferring their licked tongues upon stainless bridges. Redeeming their lot, finally. Their restricted determination! Their jam-announced destiny. The solving of the puzzling! The being of the confusion. This is what it should be? Enduring all this? This must take it out of them. Discourage them! The united bridges of the world stiff with patience. The whole striving masses! In the final battle with the vain seconds. In the close fight with the dying rules of the insignificance. Slimy body on body. The long lot of the home-comers hangs in an endless loop. In the fissure of an infinite groove. In the slice of an unreal music. Which is throttled by its noisy engine piston beating. Staccato! The shock absorbers firmly drawn. They are the bundled-up stones of blackout reactions, chained together, leading nowhere! Except to running chaos! Standing KO! Full throttling retirement! Involved in the everlasting standstill of the home-coming troublemakers. Wrapped in unpredictable jam predictions! Like the motherly break sandwich in the shine of the tin silver paper of a long gone time. Be a good boy and do not throw it into the garbage! You are a good boy. I have put my whole love into the sandwich. And covered it thick with your favourite sausage. Now go and take good care of yourself! The world out there is full of dangers! Oh, I see? So butter-bemired they hang around in my reflecting on ways out that I completely freak out about their standing still. Shock! And only make progress trembling! Shiveringjerking after shiveringjerking I move as unflashy as possible in the direction of absolutely necessary emergency exit. Actually, an impossible endeavour! Precision job! In the final stage of the mania. In the mania of the sense. In the impetuous noise of the words which I spread with shaky finger. Like a tidal wave of screaming poets. Who are closer to decay than the home-comers to the familiar home. The suction of the butter-smeared mothers. The smog of the snaky carwaves. On the thin foreskin of the Alzette which starts to wrinkle. Like the forehead of a quaint old lady who starts to brood and dreams of an excursion to the Hudson River. Of a long overdue trip through the betided sea which contracts, firmly resolved to think in peace whether it is determined to absorb the crying disgrace. That of the ageing Alzette! Which lets such a spectacle wash over it. Above it! On a knotted bridge! Above the praised end of work! To the corner of the rest, considered deserved. Which is a damn well tightened knot in the outlet model of a working day. A knot full of fear. Days full of sausage. Home-comers full of funk. Which they are now ready to share. With me! To sacrifice! To the accidental bridge conqueror. The daredevil! The one being taken in. The hanger. On this viscous strip which the home-comers themselves span onto the bridge so as not to be tempted in any way to get off lightly from the daily jam. And these with the legs in one of these flies stuck with their legs in one of these strips buzz for their one-day life and beat their wild wings, like in wedged high-capacity engines on the test bench of the global warming of the most patient minds of the civilized world. Caught with jam fairy tales, hung with car-queues! I must cop it too! Get led to believe the fairy tales. The skysick messages. Must flee into my ruin, snowed under torn-out wings and mounted with the pinched arms of a discarded Terminator. Trample above their still life. As if no other choice remained to me! And in the armoured baggage train of thoughts of my longing after more in this too much of the crowded boredom, this troublemaker of my spontaneously seized walk across the Adolphe Bridge, I must accelerate quite a lot to even use this one low chance which arises to me to outwit it. To transfer. To cross. It, the crowd of those getting in my way. This me-exterminating endless sausage. In this bloated zenith of my harmlessly begun mental leaps into the late afternoon hours. But how? Back-flying? Blurring traces? Spreading ambiguities? Ignoring rules? Clearing prejudices? Eradicating skysick wings? Ignoring the home-comers? Skipping the jam? Despising the vice squads? Which stand at the end of the nodal points of the Adolphe Bridge. Like warning twin towers. Pitifully collapsing fine dust storms. Anthropomorph ones. Me-exterminating ones! (Oops! snivel!).... And are ready to prepare the promised end for my armoured overflight. (Steep! Yeah!).... Ridiculous, inspired armour-me! Fit for scrap sublimating of a hopeless disposal attempt. Of my unclearly thought dustiness. The best-before date of my mistakes gets closer! The fingernails beg for mercy. The typed ant legs amputate my sentences. The stressed-out home-comers are firmly resolved to stop it. The torn ant wings fly over the hopeless Alzette Valley. Meekly! Flappings of hummingbirds' wings! The ready-to-fire-ending is about to fold. Only time is vital. Alone with itself! Is the only way out! As fast as possible. The decision must be made! Now! 6 pm. For eternities! From the outset! Since I have penetrated unauthorizedly. Into the waste of the seconds which have got stuck in the balustrade of the Adolphe Bridge. Like the viscous tears of a blind poet stomping around who has had rollingly enough to make him stop laughing. At the attempt to catch his death? A last time! In a bitter jump into the awry water of the Alzette? It requires no aimless explanation not to understand it! All waters of this world are awry! I do not understand it myself. What happened. What is awry! About this time. Which is not able to pass dead-straight. Second by second! Two time spots equal a straight line! Just like that! As if nothing had happened. No depression above the Cologne Bay. No high on the Alzette. No weather forecasts. No jam announcements. No bridging walk. No drawn lot. No fictitious trip to New York. No troublemakers crept away in home-comers. No armless Terminator. No impregnated lady in the car behind. No squatted Brooklyn Bridge. By no long ladies' legs. Enough fun! These legs are shaved. I no longer have the feel of them! The length of time! It slips away! They! It! The pursuing of the unclear thoughts. The striving for ways out. The overtopping of the passageways. The bending of the bridges. The pinching of the seconds. The lurching about obstacles. The preventing of the disturbing factors. All of it! Too much! Too far! The hopeless scribbling of the story. It slithers. From my fingers! The jam shows its freaky side. Is a nuclear fissioned intention. A grinning one! The jumped sentence is a venture. Which cannot decide any more! What it should boot? Into which knots it should rush? To whom it should report what! All this is sure to make you dizzy! With this jam of words chained together. Which mean little. Which still cannot free themselves. From the pressure of time. That is the way it looks! Delivering! Bridging! Filling! Emptying! A thrilling fight! Excessive hardness! Unfair word play! Penalty time announced! Measured speed excess! In the course of the race! Of the things! Exactly the neglected fraction of one second faster than the future. Caught red-handed! The time? 6 pm. From the outset! If I consider what could still come? How it stares at me? From over the end of the bridge! The bottleneck of Adolphe! In a crept-away bridge! An endless end. Without hole! Nothing happens anymore! Nothing stirs. Deathly stillness! Home-comers pegging out! Tunnel-visioning I overthrow my downfall on its terrible awaiting. That of the gathered home-comers. That of their outstretched fingers! That of their diplomatic arrogance. HE COMES! THERE! HE DARES! HE WILL SEE! WE WILL SHOW HIM! And under my cooking feet there vibrate the cars standing still. The bridge dildo starts to swing. There! Here! There! Here! The crumbling starts to take itself seriously. The stones sneak the dust. The ants leave the sinking dream ship of my sealed hopes. There is no escaping from this theater! The blasé head slaughterer glides into his comfortable box armchair and allows the spectacle to begin like crazy. The curtain rises. The Alzette Valley burns its castles. The concert of the horns throws its sound waves into these flames. The background music turns out cacophony! The chosen hero enters the stage. The jam-announced drama immediately starts in the middle of the last sentence of the events. And right away the lumpy bloodlettings of the dreamer flow inexorably into the knotty ends of the sausage. The curtain falls! The applause keeps within limits. The game is over! The audience is disappointed. The time has come! Concisely! Ripe! The knots contract. Like a satisfied dick. As always! As usual! The narrowness of the sausage becomes unfathomable. Embarrassed, the Alzette creeps away into the bum-crack of the Petrusse. The sea does not take this sight and evaporates in my sweat pearls which give a shit about the fact that the setting sun switches on its nebulous light. So that I do not ram them likewise into misfortune. Out of revenge! By mistake! Out of fury! On the bridge of the died dreams. I roll up the sleeves of my stolen arms. I am ready to fight. To die! They do not get me alive! I am and remain the chosen one. I have drawn my lot by the tail! Confound it! I will redeem it! Basta! Will torment myself across there and read the riot act to the home-comers once and for all. The self-written one! I will jump headlong into the gaping mouths of surprise. Quoting myself! My best sentences! To lead them completly astray.

To befog! To paralyse them! Will substitute offences of the seconds. Exchange earlier with later. Torment right answers with wrong questions. What should this become? What does he want to tell us? For thinking home-comers it will be hard to fight me. Gaping troublemakers will be a piece of cake in my high-carat arrogance. What are you looking at? Because I must cross these knots, I will respect no more limits, obey no more rules. Over and done! In the sausage meat of the custom fanatics I will be the dust particle of contention on which they should break their gleaming spoiler teeth. The head slaughterer will maybe applaud bored? Let him! I will be prepared for it. I will be enough thankful audience to myself. Especially in the intolerable scrum of an obdurate Adolphe Bridge! One bombed with the sudden shaking inspirations of an irritated stroller. The bridge of an undecided story. The way is clearly marked. It misleads! Still I do not anticipate, in which mis-direction exactly. How it will look. The end! Of this sausage! The last sentence! The last step! The entry into the everlasting reasons of my useless hunt for movement. For change. For astonishment. Enthusiasm. Unpredictability! The opening of the barricaded senses. The unleashing of the insoluble knots. The final bursting of the rotten sausages. The dissolving of the puzzling jam. The delivering from the tiresome troublemakers. It is unpredictable! However, time leaves me no other choice! Than to make it. To have to do it. To try it. Who should hinder me in it? You? Your tired eyes? Your misunderstandings? Your nonsense for nonsense? The ants leg bridge between us both is just a cheap sausage too. A typed end. Of the literal world. A read rage! Drawn-out ordeal. Spit-clue? Kiss-slime-trace? Eye-catcher-net? Total Springer? But, in any case, a congested imposition! Bullshit! Hopeless monologue! Stop! Let us stop it! FREEZE! You first! I cannot do it yet! Must still distribute the last sentences! In the sausage buried ones. Have at least another ten steps to go. Must throw down ballast. As much as possible. Become lighter. More ready to jump. More aggressive. More casual. Not take it so seriously! Look less deeply into danger's eyes! It could bewitch me. Subdue me! Act as if I was not concerned. Not meant! Included by pure coincidence. In the overexcited braid of this story. Only a whistling stroller. An invincible one. On the aberrational way to New York. Over there! In the friendly office. Of the drawn-out trips. Because of the special offers. Because of the storically significant slogans. Because of the feigned change. I empathize, nevertheless. I am present! Because of the shaven ladies' legs. Which on running-out day models like this one are bringing a little bit of tingling excitement into the lame features of late home-comers and lost strollers. And which animate imagination. As long as they do not stop and break. This theater of parawars! Like the pillars of an ailing Adolphe Bridge. Which never planned to make progress. Never! And will never cross another valley than that of the Alzette. If at all! Will never see the Hudson River. Not to speak of the sea! About which the longing sweat of these dripping legs can only dream in the slightest. And only if they fall in trance. The drops! By chance caught and enjoyed by someone like me. In a looking-up flight of good mood and nonchalance. On one of these wretched bridges of breathlessness. Of the thirst for more! This transition of the Alzette Valley into the home-coming end of the world. Which daily blows around my ears. Jam punctually! Properly! Annoyingly! And all that is predicted. Declared. Jam announced! Certainly! As certainly as I move hotfoot towards it. Towards this stuck knot at the other end of the Adolphe Bridge. Look it deeply in the eyes. Avoid, smart and without rushing, its uncontrolled arm movements. Squeeze myself through this knot like the knotty guide through this story. Excuse me! May I pass by? And nothing happens! Nothing! Nobody holds me back! Nobody stabs me in the scarred back! Nobody bumps into me! Nobody looks me in the eyes! They let me pass through as if nothing was really endless. Nothing important enough. None of it forever all of it! And barely have I perforated the intestinal skin of this knot and, finally, put a foot behind the jam, I am carried away by an inconceivable mash. Sink into the stream of the running-out jam. And steal a last, leaving glance at this sausage. The end. The world.